Murder in the Milk Case

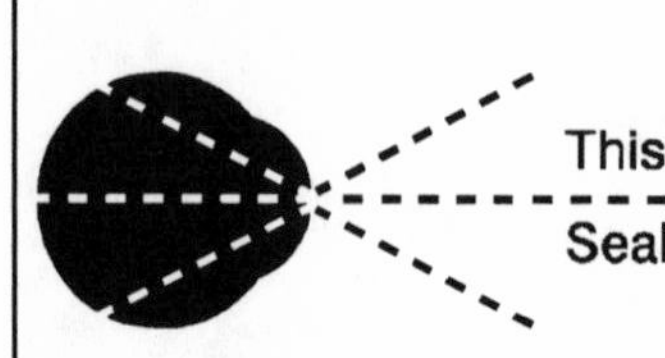

This Large Print Book carries the
Seal of Approval of N.A.V.H.

MAYHEM IN MARYLAND, BOOK 1

MURDER IN THE MILK CASE

A ROMANTIC MYSTERY

CANDICE SPEARE

THORNDIKE PRESS
A part of Gale, Cengage Learning

Detroit • New York • San Francisco • New Haven, Conn • Waterville, Maine • London

Thorndike Press, a part of Gale, Cengage Learning.

Thorndike Press® Large Print Christian Mystery.
The text of this Large Print edition is unabridged.
Other aspects of the book may vary from the original edition.
Set in 16 pt. Plantin.
Printed on permanent paper.

LIBRARY OF CONGRESS CATALOGING-IN-PUBLICATION DATA

Speare, Candice.
Murder in the milk case / by Candice Speare.
p. cm. — (A romantic mystery mayhem in Maryland ; bk. 1)
ISBN-13: 978-1-4104-1935-4 (hardcover : alk. paper)
ISBN-10: 1-4104-1935-5 (hardcover : alk. paper)
1. Housewives—Fiction. 2. Murder—Investigation—Fiction. 3. Suburban life—Maryland—Fiction. 4. Maryland—Fiction. 5. Large type books. I. Title.
PS3619.P3735M87 2009
813'.6—dc22 2009019758

Published in 2009 by arrangement with Barbour Publishing, Inc.

Printed in the United States of America
1 2 3 4 5 6 7 13 12 11 10 09

Many thanks to everyone who made this book possible: Brad Speare for always believing, not to mention putting up with my tunnel vision; Elizabeth Grosskopf and Thelma Mills for thinking I'm the best; Diana Blessing for the brainstorming; Bryon Miller, who let me see behind the milk case; Scot Hopkins, eighteen-year police veteran, who generously shared his expertise in law enforcement and went out of his way to help me with the corpse thing and Maryland law; Tamela Hancock Murray, my agent, who took a chance with a novice; and Susan Downs, my editor and friend.

1

Death wasn't normally on my mind in the grocery store parking lot. Today, however, my thoughts lingered on the untimely demise of our pet hamster. Not due to excessive amounts of grief but because I didn't have to remember to buy hamster food. Now I could concentrate on more important things — like milk.

After parking in front of the Shopper's Super Saver, I climbed from my SUV. A strong spring breeze whipped through my hair as I searched in vain for my grocery list. As usual, I had misplaced it. I tried to assemble another one in my head, but the sound of loud male voices distracted me.

I squinted in their direction. Next to a side entrance to the store, I saw Daryl Boyd, the assistant manager and an old high school acquaintance, in an intense conversation with a balding man in a blue sports jacket. Well, perhaps intense conversation wasn't an apt description. Both men's fists were balled at their sides. Daryl took a swipe at the other man, who ducked, just missing what would have been a whopping black eye. The last time I'd witnessed so much machismo had been between two fathers on the sidelines during a high school football game.

I shifted, trying to see more clearly. The men noticed me and stopped yelling. My own temper flared when I realized the identity of the man in the sports coat: Jim Bob Jenkins, the pharmacist. Today was supposed to be his day off, which was one reason I'd picked this morning to shop. He stared at me, hands on hips, then marched back inside, followed closely by Daryl, who had started yelling again.

I leaned against the SUV, asking God to help me fight my warring emotions. The good Trish against the bad Trish. Truthfully, there's nothing I like better than a fight — something I'd been known to participate in myself when I was young, much to my parents' chagrin. I was a true rough-and-ready redneck tomboy. Underneath, I guess I still am. And I especially like fights when the bad guy gets what's coming to him. That's what made my conflict of conscience so hard today. And why I needed to pray.

As far as I was concerned, Jim Bob deserved to be decked. I wanted to do it myself when, during a quarrel over a prescription, he'd hissed a threat in my ear about something in the past. I didn't believe he'd meant it — until he'd come by the office the next Friday and reminded me. I got mad and yelled at him. I told him he was wrong. He smirked and said he'd be back after I had time to reconsider what he'd said.

Right now, I wanted to go home, but I needed to shop because today was my day off. With one more glance at the door where the men had disappeared, I headed for the store. At least customers were sparse on a Monday morning, which made shopping easier. I grabbed my cart, passing through the Easter displays, trying to ignore the dread in my stomach that I might see Jim Bob. After putting a couple of impulsive candy purchases in my cart, I headed for the deli to get some coffee, one of my favorite parts of shopping.

Unfortunately, when I got there, the self-serve pump thermoses that normally held my favorite beverage were nowhere in sight. And no one was in the deli. I tapped my fingers on the glass counter, wondering why they didn't have a little bell I could bang in frustration. Meats, cheeses, and salads were still covered. Opaque plastic covered the huge slicing machines, and several knives lay next to the sink.

"Hello?" I yelled.

"Trish?"

I turned around and saw Daryl there in his red jacket, holding a hammer. His brown hair was slightly askew, probably from his run-in with Jim Bob.

"Hi, Daryl. I need coffee bad."

"We had two deli employees call in sick. Stomach bug. They're working on getting someone else in here." He sighed. "This hasn't been a good morning."

"No, I guess not," I said. "I saw you in the parking lot."

His face darkened. "No one has had any peace since that man —"

"Daryl? Oh, hey, Trish."

We both turned. Lee Ann Snyder stood in the doorway between the back room and the deli, her black hair pulled back in a ponytail. She was younger than me by two years. Back when we'd both been in 4-H, I'd taken her under my wing. "We gonna get some work done today?" she asked. "Frank is hyperventilating."

"Isn't that normal for Frank?" I'd known the store manager for years.

Daryl smirked and glanced at me. "Well, I

can't disagree, but anyway, I'm sorry about the deli. We'll have somebody here as soon as possible to get things up and running."

He said good-bye and went into the back of the store, followed by Lee Ann, who gave me a backward wave. With time marching on, I decided not to wait. Problem was, I had no grocery list. And without caffeine, I had no brain with which to think. That meant I'd have to guess what I needed. I mulled over the produce, finally settling on bananas, apples, potatoes, and a selection of salad fixings. Then I wheeled up and down the aisles, tossing in boxes and cans of stuff. Distracted only once by the books and magazines, I selected several. I love magazines with recipes in them.

At that point, I had to use the ladies' room. I didn't want to. Unlike some stores that have official customer restrooms, these are in the bowels of the building, reached only by going through two thick, swinging doors next to the meat case, then into a back room. I parked my cart and proceeded to the back, following a winding path between towering piles of cartons and cases. I didn't like being back there even when it was well lit, but today the lights were dim.

As I hurried along, clicks from my shoe heels echoed in the cavernous space, and I had visions of scary monsters from B-movies slipping out from behind boxes and stealthily dogging my steps. Monsters are the only things that frighten me, and that was my fault. When I was a teenager, I'd watched every horror flick known to man — unbeknownst to my poor parents who struggled to keep me in line. Every frame of those films was etched in my memory, ready to leap to the forefront at the slightest opportunity. Like right now. Only the distant sound of human voices kept my palms from sweating.

The beige-, brown-, and white-tiled bathroom was too warm and smelled of bleach and heavy-duty floral room deodorizer. While I was in the stall, the bathroom door opened, but no one came in. When I was done, I quickly washed my hands and rushed out the door, back into the storeroom. I heard a bang behind me, jumped, and turned, half expecting to see a slavering beast straight from my movie-fed imagination. But all I saw was a glimpse of red, followed by a whisper of a sound I couldn't identify. Then nothing. I whirled around and hurried on, ignoring the bristling of hair on my neck and the feeling that I was being watched.

When I reached the double doors, they

were moving on their hinges as if someone else had just passed through them. With relief, I pushed them open and saw a red-jacketed man hurrying up a store aisle. I'd recognize that Jack Sprat body anywhere. Frank Gaines, the store manager, otherwise known as "Dudley Do-It-All-Right," so named in grade school after the Canadian Mounties cartoon character Dudley Do-Right. Seeing him made everything feel okay again. Frank was annoying and obnoxious, but he wasn't a monster.

I grabbed my cart and hurried to finish shopping, hoping I wouldn't run into Jim Bob. Meat was next. As I stood pondering hamburger, I glanced through the glass windows into the meat-cutting room. A door to the room opened, and Lee Ann walked in. She looked up, saw me, and gave me a tepid wave. This year, we'd seen more of each other. Her daughter, Julie, was my stepdaughter's best friend. I smiled and proceeded to choose meat that I hoped I didn't have at home in the freezer. Then I hurried on to the milk case. There I opened the glass door, grabbed three gallons, and turned to leave, but the hand behind the milk had already caught my eye. It just took a minute to move along my optic nerves to my brain.

No way, I told myself as I peered back into the dairy case. There couldn't possibly be a hand behind the 2 percent milk. Surely this was a hallucination. I blinked. Twice.

Nope. Not a hallucination. A hand lay in the back of the same slot from which I'd pulled the milk. It had to be a joke. Maybe some kids had put it there.

I felt the hand and knew right away it wasn't rubber. I don't know how I knew. Reaching out and touching someone has a whole new meaning for me now. The closest I've come to dead people is reading mystery books and viewing a weekly forensic show while I fold laundry.

I felt nauseated but pulled out a few gallons of regular milk that obscured my view. I stuck my head in the dairy case for a closer look, and the cold metal racks bit into my chest. Chilly air assailed my face, temporarily removing the nausea. A little voice in the recesses of my mind screamed that a normal woman would immediately call for help. Not me. I had to investigate.

Sure enough. The hand was attached to an arm.

It made sense in a macabre way. There was no blood on the hand, which there would have been had it been separated from its arm. At least if it were fresh. I guess.

I squinted to see into the cold room behind the dairy case. In my peripheral vision, I thought I saw a flash of red, but the realization that the arm was attached to a man's body distracted me. He was sprawled over a six-wheeled cart, positioned in a way that would be terribly uncomfortable for someone alive. A familiar bald head dangled, facing away from me, and a large knife protruded from his white-shirt-clad stomach.

I had run into Jim Bob, all right. But I doubted I'd ever run into him again.

I averted my eyes, feeling a sense of unreality. The nausea returned with a vengeance. About that time, I sensed a presence behind me — mostly from all the noise he made clearing his throat. I guess I did look pretty strange with my upper body stuffed in the dairy case and my derriere sticking out in the aisle.

"Ma'am, may I help you?"

I jerked my head out so quickly I hit it on the rack. When I turned, Frank Gaines was staring at me with a puzzled look on his face.

"Trish. I didn't recognize you. What in the world are you doing?"

"Hi, Dud— Frank." I swallowed hard, grateful that I hadn't had coffee at the deli.

"Did you know Jim Bob Jenkins is in the milk case?" I glanced back where I'd seen the pharmacist, and then once again faced Frank.

"Excuse me?" Frank managed to look gallant and disbelieving at the same time.

"Jim Bob is in the milk case," I repeated.

"I'm sorry," he said in the same calm tone that annoyed me when we were in school together. "I must have misunderstood you." He smiled and nodded, as though we shared a joke. "I thought you said that Jim Bob Jenkins is in the milk case."

"I did."

"You did?"

"I did." I turned to peer into the case one more time on the off chance that I was delirious. I wasn't.

"That's really not funny, Trish. You shouldn't joke about things like that." He shook his head as if I were a wayward child.

I turned back to him, wanting to slap him. "I am not joking. Jim Bob is in the milk case. With a knife in his stomach." I said the words very slowly, as I do with my younger stepson, Charlie.

It was as if someone pushed a button and turned Frank on. His perfect, plastic manager look disappeared, and a series of expressions crossed his face, the likes of which I'd never seen there before. Each muscle in his face twitched. He pushed me out of the way to look and stuck his head in the racks, messing up his perfect hair. Then he promptly fell to the floor in a dead faint.

An hour later, I sat on an orange plastic chair in the employee lunchroom, twisting my hands in my lap. The police left me alone for a moment, no doubt to gear up for more questions. I'd called Max, my husband, who was in the midst of a meeting two hours away. He said he would leave as soon as possible. He reminded me that he played baseball with the detective who was questioning me and expected I'd be treated well. I'd seen the detective around myself, but never in a situation like this. Max sounded slightly annoyed with me. At least I wasn't calling from the emergency room — a place I ended up more times than I like to admit, after doing things that a woman my age probably shouldn't — like skateboarding.

The pungent odor of old coffee baking in a carafe in a little kitchenlike corner of the room mixed with the more pleasant smell of popcorn. I glanced around the blue-walled room for what seemed like the millionth time. A pile of certificate frames lay stacked on the gray counter, along with an open toolbox, one with molded indentations for each tool. I loved tools and wanted to see exactly what was there, but several deputies in uniforms, plus the detective, whose last name was Scott, had ordered me to sit and stay. They had isolated a number of people in different locations, and I was sure they meant every word they said.

I crossed my legs and wondered how long it would take for word to get out to the general population of Four Oaks that Trish Cunningham, a.k.a., the woman who is always in trouble, had found a body. And not just any body. Jim Bob Jenkins, the pharmacist. Murdered. With a knife in his gut.

My stomach turned over. In an effort to forget the dead man, I turned my attention again to the tools. The hammer was missing. I wondered if that was the one that Daryl had been carrying. I paused midthought and planted both feet on the floor. Had I told the detective about the hammer? I wasn't sure. Did it matter? And then there were the knives next to the sink in the deli. Had I mentioned those? The events of the morning had taken on a dreamlike quality, melting together in a collage of scenes that had no particular order.

Was there anything else I hadn't told him?

I heard footsteps outside the door. A deputy stepped into the room. He resembled Santa Claus, minus the beard, but I knew from speaking with him earlier that he was a hostile alien impersonating the merry Christmas elf.

"Mrs. Cunningham, Detective Scott wants to talk to you again. He'll be here in a moment."

"Okay." I bit my lip. I wasn't feeling well. I was tired. I just wanted to go home.

He stood by the door, arms clasped in front of him, studying me as if I were a splotch of something unpleasant on a microscope slide.

After two seconds, the silence was unbearable.

I met his gaze head-on. "So, are you guys done yet?"

He averted his eyes. "No, ma'am."

I frowned at him. "Well, what all do you have to do? I mean, how long does this take, anyway? Is it like hours or all day or what? I want to go home. Sammie, my daughter, is in kindergarten. She'll be home at lunchtime."

His bushy eyebrows edged up his forehead as his glance swept over me. "Um, well, I understand, ma'am, but we have to investigate 'til we're satisfied. You can go home when Detective Scott says you can."

"Well, I should call my car pool partner. I don't want Sammie dropped off if I'm not there." I crossed my legs again. "Is this like one of those forensic shows where crime-scene cops crawl all over the place with chemicals and cameras and stuff? Using tweezers and tape? And what about Jim Bob, er, the body, uh, the corpse. Who takes care of him? Is there a morgue van that carries him — the body — away?"

"Everything's under control, ma'am," the deputy mumbled.

"What does that mean?" I asked.

He shook his head slightly. "Just what I said."

"Oh." I sighed. "I get it. You can't tell me anything. Like on television. Everyone's a suspect until proven innocent. I found the murdered man. I'm at the top of the list. Hey, I've watched reruns of *Columbo* and *Murder She Wrote.* I know how it is."

His mouth opened and closed a few times, but he was spared answering by the entrance of Detective Eric Scott, who wore a suit. While he wasn't an alien, the detective had lost any sense of humor he might have had, and I had yet to see him smile.

After glancing at me, the detective turned

to Santa Cop. "Fletcher? Everything okay here?"

Did he think I was going to threaten the deputy with bodily harm? All one hundred pounds of me? Or did he think I had suddenly confessed to murdering Jim Bob? I eyed Santa Cop who eyed me.

"Things are fine, Sarge," he said.

"Good." Detective Scott turned his enigmatic gaze on me. "Mrs. Cunningham, I'd like to go over your statement again, if you don't mind."

And if I did mind, would I be hauled off to jail? Feeling irritable, I wondered if imprisonment would be a better alternative than answering a million questions. I decided *No* and nodded. "Fine. Go ahead."

"Please tell me again what you did from the time you arrived in the parking lot."

I proceeded to do so. They were checking their notes. When I got to the part about having to use the bathroom, both men jerked their heads up and stared at me.

Detective Scott's lips narrowed. "Mrs. Cunningham, you said nothing about this earlier."

"I didn't?" I tried to remember. "Well, it's all very confusing. I mean, I had no list and I didn't have any coffee."

"What?" the detective asked.

I shook my head and stared at the ceiling, trying to think. "Well, I really don't know what to say. There were the knives in the deli. And Daryl's hammer." Was there anything else I'd forgotten? I met both their gazes. "Did I tell you about those things?"

I had never experienced stares and vibes quite like those emanating from the two officers who stood across the room from me. I felt much worse than something icky on a microscope slide — more like a butterfly pinned alive on a display board.

Detective Scott slapped his notebook shut. "Mrs. Cunningham, we need to continue this interview at the sheriff's office."

My mouth fell open. The sheriff's office? I shivered, feeling like I'd been dropped into a play where all the cast members knew their parts but me.

Detective Scott noticed. His expression softened a fraction. "This is just normal procedure, ma'am. We'll drive you. And while you're there, I'll see to it that you speak to a victim advocate."

Before I could ask who that was, he had turned to the deputy.

"Fletcher, get her ready to go downtown. You can take her. Get her whatever she needs."

"You got it, Sarge."

Detective Scott left the room. Fletcher and I exchanged glances. For just a second, I thought maybe I saw a glimpse of compassion in his eyes. Then he motioned at the table.

"Grab your purse, Mrs. Cunningham. I'll show you to my car."

I snatched up my purse and hung onto it like it was a life preserver.

2

At the sheriff's office, Fletcher escorted me into a room barren of anything but a table and chairs for my first-ever police interview. He seemed resigned to my chatter, which is always worse when I'm nervous. He got me a cold bottle of water, and while I yammered on, he kept eyeing me when he thought I wasn't looking at him. That encouraged me to keep on talking, although after I called him Deputy Fletcher several times, he informed me that he was a corporal, not a deputy. When I asked his permission to make a phone call to arrange for Sammie to be taken care of, he agreed with alacrity, probably relieved that I'd be babbling at someone else.

That was the extent of our conversation because while I was on my cell phone, a well-dressed, proper young woman walked into the room. I hung up, and Corporal Fletcher introduced her as the victim advocate; then he left. For some reason, I found myself wanting the big man to stay. Maybe it was one of those captor/captive brainwashing things that happens to kidnapping victims. He'd been nice to me, so I felt pathetically grateful.

The advocate seemed very concerned about my well-being, asking me about my distressing experience and assuring me that she would do whatever she could to help me through this difficult time. "After all," she said, "finding a body is very, very disturbing."

No joke. I nodded and smiled as she spoke, only responding with yep or nope when I had to. Call me suspicious, but I didn't believe that she was on my side. In fact, I wanted Corporal Fletcher to come back. At least he was obvious about how he felt.

When she left, Detective Scott joined me. He greeted me with a polite, professional smile, inquiring after my well-being. I didn't bother to tell him that my well-being would be better if I never saw him or another law-enforcement officer again the rest of my life. He informed me that our interview would be taped. Then, question by question, he grilled me. Not a moment of my time at the store was left out. He even wanted to know what I'd done in the bathroom. I laughed. My first good chuckle of the day. He wasn't amused.

When we were finished and I had signed my official statement, Detective Scott wanted someone to drive me straight home. I assured him I was going to be okay. I just wanted someone to take me back to my SUV, which was still in the grocery-store parking lot. He frowned at me. I wasn't sure why. Worry? Or maybe suspicion because I wasn't collapsed in an emotional heap? Now that I thought about it, when I made that unfortunate run to the ladies' room, I could have stabbed Jim Bob. And I suppose that my own reaction, or lack thereof, when I found Jim Bob could be a sign of guilt. I hadn't fainted like Frank. Did Detective Scott think an innocent woman would have overreacted and at least screamed? The thing he didn't know was that I'd been raised on a farm. Though finding a dead person is distressing, death doesn't surprise me like it might someone who's never dragged a dead cow from a field on a chain behind a tractor.

A young, clean-cut deputy drove me back to the store. He waited until I unlocked my van before he took off. While I fumbled with my key in the ignition, I heard a tap on my window and looked up. Frank Gaines stood there. I hadn't realized he'd returned. He'd been taken to the sheriff's office for an interview, too, and crime-scene people closed the store pending collection of evidence.

I rolled down the window. His crisp, red jacket, complete with a bright yellow store logo, looked garish in the sunlight.

"What did you tell them?" he demanded, not wasting a breath on civilities.

"Hello, Frank," I said. "How are you?"

He snorted. "How do you think I'm doing? What a stupid question. Anyway, what did they ask you?"

Frank and I had had some confrontations when we were kids because of his obnoxious personality. So I decided if he was going to be unpleasant right now, I would be, too. Not the godly response, but I was past irritable and into serious grumpiness. I wanted to annoy someone. I stared at him with a purposefully vacuous, dumb-blond look. "They who?"

The muscles in his jaw worked, and a red flush crawled from his neck to his cheeks like a rash. That concerned me. I didn't want him to die of a coronary. All we needed was another body at the Shopper's Super Saver.

"Oh, you must mean the cops?" I asked innocently.

He glared down at me. "Who else?"

Even if I were going to tell him, which I wasn't, my brain had shut down. I'd be lucky to find my way home, let alone speak coherently.

"Well?" he asked impatiently, glancing at the squad cars still parked in the lot.

"I don't know."

"What?" He stared at me, looking ready to explode. "How can you not know?"

Would it be possible to carry on a whole conversation with one-syllable words?

Tiredness enveloped me like the proverbial shroud. I didn't have the energy to continue messing with his head, so I dropped my stupid act. "Look, Frank, I'm tired and crabby. I can't think. I'm liable to say something I don't want to if I continue talking. I'm positive they didn't ask me anything they didn't ask you." I turned the key in the ignition.

He gripped my windowsill. "Can't you just —"

"No, I can't," I snapped. I wished he would go away. Would I be hauled to the sheriff's office again if I ran over his toes?

He didn't move. I looked up at his face. The redness had subsided, and his expression was smirky, a look that I recognized from years of attending school with him — starting with kindergarten. I call it his tattletale face. His biggest claim to fame had been telling on people. Mostly for purposes of payback. A lot of people outgrow their juvenile behavior. Not Frank.

He leaned down, and I could see the hairs in his nose. "You had a huge fight with Jim Bob last week, remember?"

I glared at him. "I wouldn't call it huge."

Frank laughed, but not pleasantly. "You threatened to get his license as a pharmacist taken away. Everyone heard you within a mile radius."

"Yeah? And so what, anyway?" Oh, that sounded adult. I guess in terms of outgrowing juvenile behavior, I couldn't throw stones. Still, he had a point. I had argued with Jim Bob. And I hadn't told Detective Scott about it.

"Didn't Jim Bob see you again after that?"

I blinked. How did Frank know that? Then I wanted to kick myself. His smirk grew. He knew he'd scored a hit. "The cops need to know everything you know. For purposes of finding motivation for the killing. That's what they told me."

I doubted the cops told Frank anything. I shrugged, refusing to wilt under his implied threat even though I was close to hyperventilating. Motivation was a word that scared me. Mostly because I had plenty of it.

He smirked again and backed up, giving me a tiny little wave before he turned around and walked away. I asked the Lord to forgive me even while I thought how nice it would be to plant a foot hard on Frank's behind. As I pulled from the parking lot, I knew I hadn't heard the last of my unfortunate encounters with Jim Bob.

I slouched on the overstuffed, denim-covered couch in the family room. Max had called. I whined about how I'd wasted all that time shopping and didn't even get to bring my groceries home. He listened sympathetically and promised to pick up some milk.

I shivered and yanked a crocheted afghan from the back of the couch and wrapped myself up in it. Sammie was in her bedroom with enough soda, potato chips, and chocolate chip cookies to put a healthy person in a diabetic coma. I'd done that out of desperation to be alone. Poor kid would be bouncing off the walls in an hour.

When I'd picked her up from my car pool partner's house on the way home, the woman handed me Sammie's backpack and said in a stage whisper, "I didn't tell her about what's happening, but I'm going to tell my kids tonight. I'm sure it'll be all over the kindergarten class and the school tomorrow." No doubt. I was sure that my latest misfortune would be all over Four Oaks by dinnertime.

My Bible and the cordless phone sat on the end table, along with my latest mystery from the library. I glanced at them but didn't think I'd be able to concentrate because my mind was running amok. I thought about calling Abbie, my best friend, but I didn't want to talk. I had some serious thinking to do. Finding a murdered man was bad. But worse, I had known him and disliked him. In fact, if I were honest with myself and God, I felt a sense of relief that Jim Bob wouldn't be around to threaten me anymore. Now how could I reconcile that feeling with what should be grief that a man had died?

I reached for my Bible, running my fingers over the worn leather cover. It was my lifeline. At my most helpless times, just holding it gave me comfort. But that didn't happen today. The guilt was too strong. I was thinking hateful thoughts, reduced to quibbling with Frank, and I hadn't told Detective Scott about my argument with

Jim Bob. That alone would give me enough motivation to be at the top of his suspect list. Even Max didn't know, because I needed to find out if what Jim Bob had said was true.

The phone rang. Unfortunately, the caller was my mother. I love my mother, but I like to be prepared for the conversational assaults that often occur when we talk.

"Hi, Ma." My voice was tense, and I tried to relax.

"Well, I would have thought you would call me first," she said. "I had to hear all the gory details from Gail's sister's neighbor. After all I've been through with you, and this is how you repay me? By not telling me things?"

"Sorry." I stared at the ceiling. I tend to avoid telling my mother most anything because it's just too hard to deal with the aftermath. Questions, sarcasm, accusations. Still, I could tell she was worried about me. "I'm fine. I'm just not thinking clearly." And that wasn't the half of it.

"Well, I guess you have good reason to not think — for once. If I'd found a murdered person, I wouldn't think, either. I mean, the pictures left in your mind would —"

"Yep, I'm just fine," I said. "Sitting here

on the couch."

"Where is Samantha?" she asked.

"In her room eating cookies and potato chips." My stomach growled, and I sat up quickly, an action I regretted. Spots in my vision made it difficult to hear my mother, an oddity for which I had no explanation.

"Cookies and potato chips? At the same time? In her room?"

I glanced at the clock. Three. "Yes."

"Well, I never! Do you do that all the time? Land sakes! That child will have clogged arteries before she's twenty if you keep that up."

This coming from a woman who sells doughnuts for a living. I braced myself for the onslaught of lecture number one thousand, three hundred, and fifty about How to Care for Children. While waiting for the tirade to end, I slowly made my way to the kitchen and heated up some coffee. Then I went to the pantry and reached behind the cans of baked beans where I'd hidden my emergency stash of chocolate. Finally, armed with a large dark-chocolate bar and a strong cup of coffee, I sat at my round, oak kitchen table with the phone resting between my head and shoulder, still listening to her with only partial attention. When my mother is on a rant, I only need to grunt now and then to keep up my end of the conversation.

". . . although I suppose the children are fine so far." She took a deep breath. "Was it really Jim Bob?"

For anyone who isn't used to her, my mother's machine-gun conversational techniques can cause mental whiplash. I've just learned to anticipate the rapid shifts in topic.

"Yep, it was Jim Bob." I stared at my coffee, trying not to remember the knife in his stomach.

"Brutally murdered?" she asked.

"Um . . . yes." *Is there any other way to be murdered?*

She clucked her tongue. "Well, I'm not surprised."

I wasn't, either, but I wondered just what my mother knew about him. I was sure that she didn't know he'd threatened me.

"Your name will be in the paper tomorrow, you know," she informed me.

I grunted. Relieved by the change of topic, I jammed another huge piece of chocolate in my mouth, followed by a gulp of coffee.

"Were you wearing nice clothes?"

"Why?" I asked with my mouth full. Isn't it enough that I always wear clean underwear because of her constant, dire warnings that I might be in a tragic accident and the rescue workers will see my underclothes?

"Why?" My mother's tone indicated I had lost my mind. "You can't be serious. Didn't someone take your picture?"

I licked my fingers. "Not that I know of." In my stomach, coffee met chocolate in what could only be called a pitched battle. "Look, Mom, I don't want to talk about it anymore. It's too gruesome. My stomach feels queasy."

"Of course it does. I'd be worried if it didn't. Finding someone you know like that would be enough to make a normal person throw up."

I swallowed hard and ignored the implication that I wasn't normal.

"But you know what they say. This, too, shall pass. Besides, it could be worse, you know. It could have been —"

"I have to go," I said, before she explained in great detail what was worse than finding Jim Bob Jenkins with a knife in him. Something like being arrested for his murder, for instance? "I'll talk to you tomorrow, okay?"

I hung up but didn't move. The last of the uneaten chocolate sat in the torn wrapper in front of me. I couldn't finish it while the rest laughed viciously at me from my stomach. That was an unexpected reaction to my favorite bad habit.

My new side-by-side, stainless steel refrigerator kicked on, and I looked toward it. The metal gleamed. I swallowed, reminded of the steel doors of the refrigerated units in morgues that I'd seen on television. I never paid close attention to the details when the shows aired. I wished I had. Where was the body from the dairy case right now? Had it begun to decay already? Was it stretched out on some cold, metal examining table with a masked and goggled doctor standing over it with a whirring —

"Mommy, how long before dead bodies smell?"

I choked on a mouthful of coffee and almost wrenched my neck turning around. Had Sammie already heard about her mother's megaexploits at the grocery store before I could tell her myself? Relief flooded through me when I saw that my precious youngest daughter held an elaborately decorated shoe box with our deceased hamster's name spelled out in glitter on the top.

"We can wait to bury Hammie tomorrow, but he might smell by then. Charlie says that soon the body will puff all up and turn black. Then beetles and flies —"

"We'll do it tonight after Daddy gets

home," I said quickly, trying not to think about her description, which was all too real for me. "Did you wash your hands?"

"Uh-huh." She met my gaze. "It's okay if we wait."

I studied her face suspiciously. Was that hope in her eyes? Did she want to see the body puffed up and, well . . . Using all my self-control, I smiled. "We'll have the funeral tonight." I pulled her close to me while I avoided the box. I didn't feel like touching another dead body, even through cardboard.

"Okay." She sighed.

"Charlie can be a little gruesome," I said.

She nodded, her little mouth pursed, brows drawn into a frown. "Yeah, Charlie sees dead people."

I know from expert opinion — mine — that the challenge of following childhood conversational twists is the leading cause of brain-cell loss in mothers. Not to mention dealing with the issues said conversations reveal.

"Charlie — sees — what?" The slowness of my speech was an outward indication of the sluggishness of my mind. Had I just heard my sweet, Christian-school-educated daughter say what I thought she said about her Christian-school-educated brother?

Sam pulled away and put her empty hand

on her mouth. "Oops. I shouldn't have told you."

Charlie has yet to learn that telling his younger sister anything is tantamount to sending a taped advertisement to the local radio station. Or telling his grandmother.

He had arrived home a couple of minutes ago. I glanced toward the doorway that led to the family room where he was watching television, his favorite activity after arguing. Dead people? I had to do something about this, but before I could try to think, the kitchen door flew open, banging against the yellow wall. Tommy, my seventeen-year-old stepson breezed in, followed by my step-daughter, Karen.

Tommy grinned with a look so reminiscent of his father that I automatically smiled. "Way cool, Mom! You're a celebrity!"

Karen crossed her arms and stared at me, saying nothing. That wasn't surprising, given she was a moody fifteen-year-old, using up her daily store of friendly conversation on the telephone with Julie Snyder, Lee Ann's daughter.

Sam watched everyone with bright eyes, distracted from planning Hammie's funeral. I was sure her active mind was already mulling over all the possible reasons for her mother's sudden notoriety. She slipped a chubby hand into mine and put her mouth next to my ear. "Mommy, what is he talking about?"

Before I could answer, the back door opened again and in walked Max. His black hair, graying slightly at his temples, ruffled from the wind, gave him the casual appearance of a wealthy man just in from yachting — something his snooty mother claimed he'd do on a regular basis if it weren't for me. As far as she was concerned, I was too much of a redneck and too young to be a good wife for Max.

He put a small plastic bag on the counter.

Sammie ran to him. "Daddy! We're going to have a funeral!"

"Dad, did you hear the cool news about Mom and the body?" Tommy said.

Karen just stared at all of us in turn with her mouth quirked in a slight sneer.

Max fielded the questions and a physical assault on his knees by Sammie with his usual aplomb.

"That's why I'm home early." He picked Sammie up and hugged her.

"Dad, did you hear —" Tommy began.

"I heard." Max looked at me. "Did you start dinner yet, honey?"

"You mean you want to eat tonight?" I joked while I tried to remember what was in the freezer.

Tommy's body vibrated with the energy only teenage boys emanate. "Yeah, but did you —"

"Why don't all of you decide what kind of pizza you'd like, call in the order, and go pick it up?" Over Sammie's head, Max put his finger to his lips. Tommy's eyes widened, and he nodded. Max wanted to wait to tell Sammie about her mother's misadventures. He kissed Sam's cheek and put her down. Then he pulled out his wallet and handed Tommy some twenties. "Let's talk about everything when you get home. Oh, and grab Charlie, too. He's probably watching television."

"I don't want to go," Karen grumbled.

Max fixed her with a level stare. "Go anyway."

As the kids trooped from the kitchen, I met Max's gaze. He closed the distance between us before I could blink, reached out for my hands, and lifted me to my feet, enclosing me in a hug. The lingering crisp scent of the aftershave he'd put on that morning smelled good. For a moment, I tried to forget everything but the feel of his body against mine and his arms wrapped tightly around me.

"There is something to be said for the old

days when a man could lock his wife away for safekeeping," he murmured in my hair.

"Very funny," I said into his shirt.

"I brought you something." He backed up, smiled, and went back to the counter for the bag, pulled out a little box, and handed it to me with a kiss. "I was saving this for Easter, but I know this was a hard day, so I want you to have it now."

I opened the box and found a tiny gold cross on a braided, gold chain. "Oh, Max, it's beautiful." I blinked back tears.

"It's to remind you of our first date."

We had our first date alone after church on Easter Sunday.

"Thank you, honey," I whispered. I pulled the delicate necklace from the box, thinking how much I didn't deserve the gift.

He helped me put it on. I turned around so he could see it. Then I looked up at him.

Worry creased his brow above his green eyes. "I sent all the kids away so we could talk. Are you sure you're okay?"

"Yes." I tried to ignore the feeling of apprehension in my stomach. Now that Jim Bob was dead, did I really have to say anything? Perhaps the past could stay in the past. I wrapped my arms around Max again and lifted my face. He kissed me, an activity that I usually enjoy more than just about anything else in the world. I almost succeeded in forgetting my day until I heard a gagging sound.

"Eeeww. Come on, you guys. Stop it."

Max and I reluctantly parted lips and turned. Charlie stood framed in the kitchen doorway, red hair stuck out at odd angles, and he had a fierce scowl on his face.

He stalked over to stand in front of us. "Why didn't you tell me about the grocery store? Mike just told me on the phone. This is important."

Max knelt in front of Charlie. "We're not going to talk about it right now. Go with your brother and sisters and pick up the pizza. We'll discuss it later."

"But, Dad."

Max stood. "Please."

Charlie's cheeks puffed up with all the words he wanted to say. Then he whirled on his heels and left the room.

My husband watched the doorway until he heard the front door slam. "Good. They're gone." He turned to me and studied my face. "You want to tell me about today?"

"Not really. I don't feel like talking about it." I had a feeling Max wanted to do more than listen. He probably had a few things he wanted to say, as well. I braced myself for his comments, which would be something along the line of "Why can't you stay out of trouble for one week?"

He shook his head. "You're sure? It's not like you not to talk."

How well he knew me — but I kept my lips zipped and nodded.

He sighed. "Of all the people in Four Oaks, why were you the one to find a body? In the milk case of all places?"

I'd been right. I stuck my chin in the air. "I didn't do it on purpose. And don't remind me of the milk case. I'll never be able to look at dairy products the same again."

"I'm sorry," he said.

I crossed my arms. "Well, at least I didn't get hurt. It's not as bad as when I tried to hog-tie that calf to prove I could, and then it kicked me. Or when I sprained my wrist skateboarding with Charlie, or the time I went rock climbing with Tommy and got stuck. Or . . ."

"Trish, honey," Max said softly.

"Yeah?"

"Please don't remind me. I worry about you as much as I worry about the kids."

I sighed in exasperation. "This isn't the same. It was someone else who got hurt." I paused. "Well, killed."

"You found him," he said.

"So you keep reminding me. Don't worry. It's over." I hoped.

He rubbed his temple. "Well, at least your part in this should be over, except that you might have to eventually go to trial or something to testify about what you saw. You should like that." He grinned slightly. He knows how much I enjoy drama and yelling.

But this time, I wasn't excited. I glanced at the floor. "Well, a trial could be fun." As long as I was a witness and not the accused.

He put his hands on my arms. "Baby, are you okay? You're not acting right."

"Yes." I wasn't quite truthful. Even the use of my pet name wasn't enough to make me feel better.

"Trish?" His concern was so evident in his furrowed forehead that I hugged him.

"Don't worry," I whispered in his ear. "It'll be okay. All's well that ends well. That's what my mother says."

"I hope so." He pulled me close. "I really, really hope so."

I did, too.

3

I woke to light shining brightly through the miniblinds on the windows. Max's side of the bed was empty. I looked at the clock. Eight in the morning. I never sleep that late.

I flung myself from the bed and ran to the bathroom. My stomach felt queasy. I hoped it was nerves and not the stomach bug from the store employees. I brushed my teeth and jerked on my fuzzy purple robe and matching slippers. Then I yanked the bedroom door open and hurled myself down the hallway — straight into Max.

He grabbed my shoulders to keep me from bouncing backwards. "Hey! Take it easy."

"Why did you let me oversleep?" I gasped, frantically trying to get loose. "What about the children?"

"All taken care of," he said.

"Breakfast?" I stopped struggling, breathing heavily.

Max loosened his grip. "Fixed and finished."

"Car pool?" My heartbeat slowed.

"Took care of it. Honey, relax. Everything's under control. You needed the sleep."

I took a deep breath and tried to think of all the things I knew I had to remember. "Four Oaks Self-Storage?"

"We both took the morning off. I told you, everything's under control." He rubbed his hands up and down my arms. "You want something to eat?" He linked my arm in his and walked me downstairs to the kitchen.

"Okay." I wouldn't argue, although I didn't feel like eating. But I did want to read the paper. I wanted to see if my picture was in there and to make sure nothing had been said to incriminate me.

He went to the refrigerator. "Eggs?"

"No, thanks." I looked around for the newspaper. "My stomach feels weird this morning. How about toast and jelly?"

A note lay on the table next to the cordless phone. *Abbie and George called* and *Grandmom got a letter from Uncle Russ* were written in different scrawls.

I held it up. "What's all this?"

"Phone calls. Russ wrote his first letter from boot camp."

My little brother, in the Navy now. And

inaccessible for weeks.

Max grabbed the bread from the bread box. "Abbie said she's coming over this afternoon. She's bringing coffee cake from your mother's shop."

My mother's coffee cake was famous, just like her doughnuts, and for good reason. And my heart warmed with pleasure at the thought of visiting with my best friend.

Max put bread in the toaster. "You sure this is all you want?"

"Yep." The morning paper lay folded on the chair where Max had been sitting. I reached over, grabbed it, and shook it open.

"I wish you wouldn't read that right now." Max was getting jelly from the refrigerator.

"I want to see if my name's in the paper," I mumbled.

The paper didn't have a picture of me, but there was a lengthy article about Jim Bob's murder. I had just begun to scan that when Max snatched it out from under me and placed my food on the table. I hadn't even seen him coming.

"Hey, you pushy man." I tried to grab it back.

"Pushy and overprotective. That's me." He grinned as he folded it and tucked it under his arm. "Maybe I am, but would you mind eating first? And would you consider reining in your inquisitive mind and just leaving the whole mess behind you?"

If only he knew that I couldn't. But before I could accuse him of chronic bossiness, as well as chauvinism, the phone rang.

I grabbed it. "Hello?"

"Mrs. C? This is Shirl."

Shirl managed the office at Four Oaks Self-Storage. She's so good at her job she never calls us at home unless something has happened.

"What's wrong?" I asked.

"That gate program isn't working again. People can't use their codes to get in. That kid Kevin who works on the weekends was having trouble, too."

I glanced at my husband who still held the paper under his arm. "You need to talk to Max."

Smiling inwardly, I shoved the phone into Max's hand. "It's Shirl." Then I snatched the paper from him.

As I smoothed it on the table, his voice rumbled in the background. I heard him say, "Just leave the gate open for now. I need to buy a new program anyway. Thank you for calling. Listen, I've got another call beeping in."

The article didn't say any more than I already knew. That was good as far as I was concerned.

The sound of Max's voice stopped. He put the phone on the table. I looked up. He was staring at me with a frown.

"What?" I asked.

"That was Eric Scott. He needs to talk to you."

I felt my heart sink to my toes, but I couldn't avoid Max's gaze. "What does he want?"

"For you to go to the sheriff's office for an interview." Max crossed his arms. "In an hour."

I glanced at the clock, feeling the weight of shame press in on me. I might not be guilty of anything as heinous as murder, but I was certainly guilty of keeping secrets.

"I have a bad feeling about this," Max murmured as he rubbed the bridge of his nose.

Me, too, and guilt made me irritable. I folded the paper and slapped it on the table. "I didn't find Jim Bob in the milk case on purpose."

"I know that, honey," Max said.

"And I didn't do it to embarrass your mother." Her kind didn't shop at the Shopper's Super Saver. Fortunately, my hoity-toity in-laws had just come back from a cruise the night before. Now they were in

Florida and weren't likely to hear by phone about how their hayseed daughter-in-law was in trouble again, until at least after brunch when their equally hoity-toity friends would have finished the morning paper — I hoped.

He took a couple of deep breaths. "I could care less what my mother thinks. I'm worried about you. You're so impetuous I don't know what you're going to do next."

Technically that was true, but I didn't want to admit it. "So then, it's not a big problem, right?"

"Your impulsiveness or the murder?" he asked.

"The murder," I grumbled. "I understand exactly how you feel about the other issue."

He walked over and kissed my forehead. "No, you don't. One of the reasons I love you so much is your impulsive nature. For a control freak like me, it's a breath of fresh air. However, it can be frightening, too, especially when there's a dead body involved."

"But finding Jim Bob Jenkins wasn't anything impulsive on my part," I said. "I didn't put him there."

"I know, I know. I just wish you weren't involved in all this." Max sighed again. "Your toast is cold. I'll make you more while you get ready to go. Then I'll drive you down there. You can eat on the way. I hope this is the last we hear about Jim Bob's murder except in the news.

Me, too. But, as my mother would say, "If wishes were horses, beggars would ride."

Once again I was shown to an interview room, but Corporal Fletcher was nowhere in sight. As I sat down, Detective Scott arrived, alone. He sat near me, at the corner of my side of the table.

"Thank you for coming, Mrs. Cunningham." He pulled a pen and notebook from his pocket.

"You can call me Trish," I said.

He nodded and met my gaze with a slight smile. "Okay, Trish. How are you today?"

"Fine." I resisted the urge to twist my hands together in my lap.

"Can I get you anything?" he asked. "A drink?"

"No, thank you." I just wanted to get this over with.

"I'd like to ask you a few more questions, if I may." He tapped his pen on the table. "How well did you know Jim Bob Jenkins?"

I shrugged, glancing at the detective, then away. "He was the pharmacist at the store. His deceased wife used to be in the garden club with my mother."

Tap, tap, tap, tap.

"So, how well did you know him?" Detective Scott's body was taut.

I shrugged again. "Like I said, he was the pharmacist at the store. I mean, how well do you get to know someone like that? Of course I did hear things from my mother about his wife. She died suddenly."

He nodded and leaned toward me. "Did you have contact with him recently?"

I ground my teeth for just a second, knowing Frank had told on me. Perhaps avoidance would work. "I know what's going on. You're wondering if I've forgotten to tell you anything else."

Tap, tap, tap, tap.

"Yes. Like, did you have any contact with Jim Bob recently?" Detective Scott's eyes bore into mine.

He wasn't going to let this go. I finally heaved a sigh. "Oh, all right. Obviously, Dudley Do-It-All-Right already talked to you. He's the biggest pain in the whole world. I thought maybe he had changed, but no. Not at all." I put my elbows on the table. "I went to school with him, you know."

The detective's eyes had widened. "Dudley Do-It-All-Right?"

"Yes. Frank Gaines. We called him that in school after that perfect Canadian Mountie guy. Frank always thought he was so above everyone, and he's a tattletale of the worst kind. I beat him up in first grade. And then in third and sixth. He's had it in for me ever since."

"I see." Detective Scott coughed and shifted in his chair. "Let's get back to my question. Did you have contact with Jim Bob Jenkins lately?"

I glanced down at the table. The detective wasn't going to let me out of this. "Yes," I mumbled, rubbing my fingers on my knees.

"Where?" he asked.

"At the pharmacy." I met Detective Scott's gaze. "Jim Bob messed up Sammie's prescription. When I discovered the mistake, I was furious. He could kill her by being careless like that."

"And what did you say to him?" The detective's tone was mild, but his eyes were sharp, watching me like a bird of prey.

"I told him I was going to report him and get his license taken away."

"Mmm." He kept staring at me. "And then what happened?"

"We had a fight." I absolutely did not want to tell Detective Scott about my deep, dark secret.

"Can you tell me about that fight?" he asked.

I glanced at the table again. "Well, we sort of worked it all out after that."

"Worked it out?"

"He, uh, stopped arguing."

"He stopped arguing," Detective Scott repeated, his eyes narrowed.

"Yes. And Frank butted in and offered me a discount on my purchases. It was like he was protecting Jim Bob or something." I met Detective Scott's eyes defiantly. I refused to say anything about Jim Bob's threats until I knew if they had basis in fact.

"Is that all?" the detective asked.

"Well, I don't remember what I bought that day or anything." I crossed my arms. "Except that I should own stock in the store because I'm there so much. However, after this, I —"

"Anything else you remember? Anything you want to tell me?"

I shook my head.

Detective Scott stared at me for a moment more, then shut his notebook, tucked it in his pocket, and stood.

"Well, that will be all today. Thank you, Trish."

I felt off balance because he'd given up too easily. As I picked up my purse, I wondered why. He opened the door for me. As I walked out to the hall, I felt his eyes on my back.

"Trish?" he said behind me.

I turned. "Yes?"

"Is this yours?" He held my cell phone in his hand.

I glanced into my purse. No phone. "Yes."

As I took it from him, he met my eyes with a slight smile and assessing gaze. "I'll be in touch."

I involuntarily shivered. That sounded a great deal like a threat.

Max and I were standing at the front door in the process of a very nice good-bye. He looked devastatingly handsome in a navy pinstripe suit that always distracted me. I ran his lapel through my fingers and wished for one whole day alone together without disruptions or the guilt I now carried.

After he thoroughly kissed me, he leaned down and picked up his briefcase. "Dad'll be home in a few days. Today I'm going to finalize plans with the architect for the new facility outside Baltimore."

Max and his father had big plans for a self-storage empire, although that was only one of their many business ventures. The fact that my in-laws were returning soon wasn't good news.

"Honey?"

I glanced up.

He brushed hair from my face. "What are you doing this afternoon?"

Was he checking up on my activities? "Well, I don't intend to find another body, if that's what you're worried about."

He inhaled. "That's not what I meant."

I relented. Inner turmoil was making me snappy. "I'm sorry. Abbie's coming over, remember? Then I'll do some bookkeeping since I didn't get to work today."

Sammie arrived as he was leaving, and they had a little powwow, apparently discussing the possible addition of another hamster to our family. She and I ate lunch together; then I got her settled in the family room, feeling guilty that I was entertaining my child with television. I could only imagine what my mother would say about that. Seemed lately that my life was one huge guilt trip.

As I made coffee in preparation for Abbie's visit, her shadow appeared at the back door, and I waved her in.

"Hey, thanks for taking a break from your writing."

"Hi, hon. No problem." She kissed my cheek and put a bag on the table. "Your mother says she never sees you anymore."

"She always says that." I pulled two mugs from the cupboard and placed them on the table.

Abbie laughed and slipped fluidly onto a chair, crossing her long legs at the ankles. The pink of her sweater shouldn't have looked good with her red hair, but on her, the effect was stunning. In her black jeans, she looked like one of the heroines in the novels she wrote. If I hadn't known her since kindergarten and loved her so much, I'd be rabidly jealous of her good looks.

"How is the book coming along?" I pulled the bag off the coffee cake. It smelled wonderful, as do all my mother's baked goods.

She laughed. "I'm at the point where my brain is fried. I needed a break."

"I can't wait to read it." I leaned against the counter. "Are you sure working at the health fair this Saturday won't be a problem for you?"

She shook her head. "Not at all. Another mental health respite. Besides, how could I break our yearly tradition?"

As I poured coffee, she watched me closely. "You okay? You look a little pale."

"Finding a body will do that." I put the carafe back on the coffeemaker and grabbed a knife from the drawer. The blade glittered in the sunlight that streamed through the kitchen windows. My mind flashed to Jim Bob's body. I put the knife on the table and shoved it toward Abbie. "How about you cut?"

She nodded and glanced at me with narrowed eyes. "Sit, Trish. You look like you're going to fall over."

I sat down and put my chin in my hands. She served both of us and then settled back in her chair. "Okay, tell me about what happened at the store."

I shook my head. I couldn't start there. I had to start earlier. "Do you remember that rash of road-sign thefts eight years ago?"

She raised her eyebrows. I jabbed my fork in the coffee cake, breaking it into pieces.

"What does that have to do with anything, especially Jim Bob's murder?" she asked.

Unwanted tears sprang into my eyes. I dropped my fork and picked up a napkin. "He was threatening me, Abbie. He said that Russ was involved in those thefts, and he was going to tell Max and his family. That gives me motive to murder Jim Bob."

She put her fork down, too. "Why in the world?"

"Because Max's wife was killed at an

intersection where a stop sign had been removed.”

4

"Oh, Trish." Abbie stared at me with wide eyes.

"Remember that big fight I had with Jim Bob at the pharmacy a couple weeks ago?" I asked.

She nodded.

"I threatened to report him to whatever board supervises pharmacists. Frank intervened, but Jim Bob told me I shouldn't throw stones." I continued to poke at my coffee cake. "I figured he was just referring to my tendency for mishaps. Well, last Friday before Shirl got in the office, Jim Bob came by Four Oaks Self-Storage. That's when he told me about the stop sign. He said if I didn't give him free storage units he was going to tell Max and his family, plus get Russ kicked out of the Navy. Involuntary manslaughter or something like that." I glanced at Abbie. "I haven't told Max yet. I need to know for sure."

She frowned. "Why can't you ask Russ?"

"Boot camp, remember?"

"Oh, yeah." She sighed. "Okay, well, do you think Russ was involved?"

"I have no idea. But I do remember when I was watching him pack I saw what could have been sheet-covered road signs in his closet." I bunched up my napkin. "You know this makes me look guilty in the cops' eyes."

She tucked her hair behind her ears. "Perhaps."

"I have a feeling that Detective Eric Scott suspects something."

She sat up straight. "So he's the lead investigator?"

I nodded. "Yeah. And this morning, I was down in the interview room for the second time. I think he knows."

Her gaze met mine. "You didn't tell him?"

I took a sip of coffee then set the cup down hard. "I sort of hoped that with Jim Bob dead no one would ever have to know."

She gazed at me with one delicate eyebrow raised. "So you're saying if they find Jim Bob's murderer today you're going to keep this a secret the rest of your life? Even from Max, and even if it's true?" She paused and tapped a finger on the table. "And if they don't find his murderer right away and you're somehow implicated in all of this, then the secret's out. Russ could be yanked out of the Navy, charged with Lindsey's death, and Max will feel like you betrayed him."

Put that way, it all sounded horrible. Was that what I was saying? Could I not tell Max the rest of my life? And if he did find out before I told him . . . I mashed a piece of coffee cake into my plate with my fingertip. "I guess I'm just scared. Sometimes it's hard enough living with what feels like the ghost of a first wife and the kids' real mother. But you're right. I'm not thinking clearly at all. I don't know what to do."

She leaned across the table. "Come on, Trish, it's not like you to be so helpless and obtuse."

Her words felt like a slap. I glared at her. "What exactly does that mean?"

She smiled serenely and leaned back in her chair. I could see cogs turning in her brain. "Seems to me you'd want to find out what you can yourself. And remember, if Jim Bob knew, then he had to have heard it from someone else. Besides, Eric isn't going to let up."

I hadn't thought about it all quite like that. Then I realized she'd used the detective's first name. "You know Detective Scott?"

"Know him?" She shrugged. "I'm not sure he's knowable. With his impenetrable stares, he's so self-contained it's annoying. He just happens to be the person I ended up with as a writing consultant. The other guy who was helping me retired and sent me Eric's way. Ironically, he doesn't seem to like my books."

Who could not like Abbie's books? "Maybe he just doesn't like to read."

"Who knows? But he's nothing if not persistent." She nibbled on a piece of coffee cake and then put her fork down, meeting my gaze with a grin. "Do you remember when we were in sixth grade and decided we were going to be the Hardy Boys — only we were girls?"

I nodded. We'd called ourselves the Hardier Girls and ordered fingerprint powder and other detective stuff from mail-order places. We spent that summer following people around, looking for crimes. My mother finally banned the two of us from using the powder in the house because it was so messy.

I frowned. "So you're saying I need to investigate?"

"You have to tell Max, Trish — sooner

than later. But it would be nice if you knew the facts. We need to look into this further. Find some answers."

"You know what?" I sat up straight. "Maybe I could find out who killed Jim Bob. Then Detective Scott would leave me and my family alone."

One corner of her mouth turned up. "That's my girl. Tell you what. I'll go to the library, look through old newspapers, and see what the articles said about Lindsey's accident. I have to go there anyway."

I nodded. Abbie took another bite of coffee cake. I didn't feel well, so I left mine uneaten.

"I'm on a deadline, so I can't help much, but this is a good plan. It'll take your mind off things and give me satisfaction."

"Satisfaction?" I asked.

"Yes." She smiled but didn't explain.

I had a feeling she wanted to one-up Detective Scott. That was fine with me, for two reasons. First, he annoyed me, too. Second, turnabout was fair play. She helped me. I could help her. My mind was already formulating ideas. "Thank you."

"What are friends for?" She held out her index finger.

I held out mine, and we touched the tips.

Our old sign of friendship. When we were

little, we'd pricked our fingers, made them bleed, and held them together. Blood sisters.

"Here's to crime solving," she said.

"Yes." I felt a stirring inside me. "Here's to crime solving."

After Abbie left, my three oldest children came home, leaving me no time to think.

Charlie grunted at me as he ran through the kitchen to the family room.

Tommy kissed my cheek as he passed through. "Hey, Mom. I'm working this evening, so I won't be here for dinner. Dad knows."

"Okay." I looked at Karen. "How was school?"

"Fine." She opened the refrigerator. "I'm going over to Julie's in a while. Tommy's taking me on his way to work."

She was spending a lot of time at the Snyders' house. Thin, sad-eyed Julie was Lee Ann's only daughter. The girls' relationship benefited my shopping. Lee Ann always clued me into the meat sales at the Shopper's Super Saver, and she didn't mind doing special cuts for me. But I was concerned about Karen. As she and Julie got closer, there was a distinct deterioration in Karen's behavior. She'd recently dropped all of her extracurricular activities, which disturbed us because she needed them to get into college. Max and I were praying for wisdom about how to handle the situation.

A long silence ensued while she rummaged through the shelves.

"I'm going to eat dinner there," she finally said.

"That's fine. Does your father know?"

She snatched a diet soda from the refrigerator, slammed the door, and turned to face me. "I'm sure you'll tell him."

Whoops. Worse than normal. Maybe she had PMS. "No doubt I will." I eyed her. "You want some chocolate?"

She put her hands on her hips. "Is that a joke?"

"Do you want it to be?"

She grabbed her pants and shook the fabric. "I don't need any more calories. I'm too tall. I'm getting fat. And I hate my hair."

Was that a slam against mine, which looked very much like hers? Long, blond, and very, very curly.

"You're lucky to be short and skinny," she said as she stomped from the kitchen.

Well, that didn't go too badly considering how things had been recently.

Strains of discordant, eerie music drifted from the family room. I peeked in. Sammie sat on the couch. Charlie was hunched two feet in front of the wide-screen television. Over his spiky hair, I saw a man dressed in a white suit, walking from the shadows, slowly filling the screen. The spooky music subsided slightly as he droned in a grim, melodramatic voice. "The accounts you will see today are real, although some of the drama is represented by actors." He paused, staring intently into the camera, which closed in on his face. Aided by makeup and lighting, his facial bones protruded, making him appear almost skeletal. "My name is Perry Mitchell. Welcome to" — he paused dramatically — *"Mysterious Disappearances."*

No wonder Charlie saw dead people. Max and I had to talk about this. "Charlie, please turn that off."

"But, Mom, I watch this over at Mike's. It's great! You wouldn't believe how many people disappear all the time. I mean, even you or Dad could be faking everything and really be serial killers."

I gazed at Charlie, disturbed and amazed at the way his brain worked. It didn't seem right for an eight-year-old kid. Besides, Sammie's rapt, openmouthed attention to Charlie's words and subsequent quizzical glance in my direction told me I'd better stop this serial-killer rumor right here;

otherwise, I'd be hearing about it from my mother.

"Don't be silly, Charlie," I said. "You know Dad and I are who we say we are — you know our parents. Now turn it off."

"But I —"

The ringing phone interrupted him.

"Maybe that's Mike." Charlie galloped to the kitchen to grab the cordless. He probably hoped that Mike would invite him over so he could watch the show there.

I heard the sound of his murmuring voice; then he bounced back into the family room. "It's Grandmom — your mother. She wants to take me and Sammie out for ice cream tonight."

Sammie squealed and clapped her hands. "Please say yes, Mommy."

"Okay." I took the phone from Charlie, turned off the television, and the two scampered out of the room. I took a deep breath and put the receiver to my ear. "Hi, Ma. That's nice of you to offer. They're excited."

"Well, I don't see any of you often enough, so I had to take things into my own hands. I love Max's children like they were my own grandchildren, you know."

I did know. About taking things into her own hands and loving Max's kids.

I dropped onto the sofa. Perhaps I could distract her. "How is Daddy doing at that sale . . . ? Where is it? Pennsylvania?"

"Yes. He bought two cows. Why we need them is beyond me. But he's worried about you. He'll be back in time for Sunday dinner. So did you work today?"

"No. I went to talk to Detective Scott. I —"

"Did you remember that Jim Bob's wife was one of my dearest, deceased friends?"

"Yes." I accepted the fact that I wouldn't get a word in edgewise, which was just as well. Then I wouldn't have to hear her interpretation of my words months later.

"It's terrible," she droned. "Horrible."

"Yes, it is." I wondered if she realized how horrible it was for the person who found Jim Bob. "When did his wife die?"

"Not long enough for him to have remarried last year, but he did anyway." The indignant tone in her voice indicated there was much more to the story. "Don't you remember that? I told you all about it."

"Well, now that you mention it," I murmured.

She sighed. "After five years — can you believe it? He had the nerve to marry again."

"Five years," I repeated. "I would think five years would be plenty of —"

"Well, that shows how much you know." She snorted. "As far as I'm concerned, he should have waited forever. What in the world does a man his age want with a woman thirty years his junior?"

Well, I could think of at least one thing.

"And not only that, he let her redecorate the house. I'm sure Estelle turned over in her grave. It's indecent. And now this. I tell you, what goes around comes around."

I chewed on my fingernail as I tried to figure out what had gone around and come back again. Then I realized I was missing a valuable opportunity to gather clues. "So Jim Bob's widow is young. . . ."

"Didn't I say that? You need to listen to me. Oops, I have a customer. Gail had to leave early for a doctor's appointment. It's been a busy day. I'll talk to you later."

The phone clicked in my ear. I sat staring at the receiver in my hand. The plot thickened, so to speak. After becoming a recluse, Jim Bob's first wife died unexpectedly. He married someone much younger. I'd think the mystery was solved. That he killed his wife in order to marry a greedy younger woman, and she, in turn, killed him for his money. Problem was, Jim Bob waited five years before he remarried.

■ ■ ■ ■

After dinner, Abbie called. She'd made copies of articles for me but hadn't learned anything that we didn't already know. She had to get back to her writing but promised to keep checking around for more information. She encouraged me to check for motivations and suggested that perhaps someone else was guilty of the road-sign thefts but pointed the finger at Russ.

I debated writing a letter to Russ at boot camp to ask him about the stop sign. That would clear things up right away, but I couldn't. Boot camp was hard enough without the added pressure of this problem. If he wasn't guilty, then he'd just sit there and worry. I glanced at the four- and five-year-old Sunday school curriculum laid out on the kitchen table. I was supposed to be preparing for Sunday's lesson. The practical part of the lesson was about a little girl who lied to her parents. I ignored the niggling of my conscience that I hadn't yet told Max about Jim Bob's threat. But I did have to figure things out first. At least that's what I kept telling myself.

Was my brother really guilty? And who had killed Jim Bob? What exactly had my mother said? I pulled a blank piece of paper from my notebook and began to doodle. Then I wrote down Jim Bob and young wife. I followed those words with MOTIVATION written in large block letters. What exactly gave someone motivation to murder? Strong emotion, like love gone wrong, or hate, or fear . . .

"Hey, baby." Max walked in the room behind me. I shoved my notes under the Sunday school lesson. If Max knew what I was doing, he'd want to know why.

He rubbed my shoulders. I leaned back and looked up at him.

"Can you take a break and come sit with me?" he asked. "We're alone."

I hadn't even thought about that, which was unusual since alone time for us was so rare, and I love spending time with him. But now that Max mentioned it, the house was quiet. Sammie and Charlie wouldn't be home for another hour. Karen was over at Julie's house, and Tommy was working.

On the couch in the family room, I nestled against Max with my head on his shoulder, trying valiantly to clear my mind.

"Isn't it nice to have all the kids in school now?" He stroked my hair. "That little kid thing is just about over."

I nodded. "Yeah, I guess. But the issues

we deal with are bigger. Like, Karen and her moodiness, and Charlie. He sees dead people."

Max laughed. "Charlie has an imagination that's almost as big as yours."

I pulled away from him. "Come on. Be serious. It worries me. I mean, we take him to Sunday school and church. He goes to Christian school. He knows there aren't any such things as ghosts. What will his teachers think? We need to talk to him."

"I don't think he really sees things." Max pulled me tight. "Now let's enjoy being alone and not talk about the kids or anything important."

I saw the gleam in his eye. "Just what did you have in mind?"

He leaned down and kissed me.

I willed myself to stop thinking. I almost succeeded, but the secret I held wouldn't be still and wiggled in the back of my brain. After a very pleasant couple of minutes, I could no longer contain my thoughts. I pulled away from him.

He frowned at me. "What's wrong?"

I glanced at his face. I'd memorized every inch of it, from his green eyes and the skin that crinkled around them when he smiled, to the scar on his cheek that he'd gotten when he was just a kid and fell off the swing set. My heart ached keeping what I knew from him, and I had to tell him.

"Max, I wanted to talk to you —"

He cupped his hand under my chin. "I don't really feel like talking."

"But —"

He kissed me again, successfully shutting me up; then the front door burst open, banging against the wall. We had barely separated lips when Karen whirled into the room.

"Dad."

I brushed hair out of my eyes, and Max adjusted his collar.

"Oh — my — stars! I can't believe you guys." She put her hands on her hips. "What if I had company?"

She didn't, but I decided not to point that out.

"What's wrong?" Max asked.

Tears welled up in her eyes. "I had to leave Julie's. Her mother kicked her father out. Julie can't stop crying, and her mother is acting all weird. There's this guy . . ." She heaved a sigh. "It's horrible. I mean, I remember when Mommy . . ." Her voice broke.

My breath caught in my throat.

Max patted the sofa next to him. "Why don't you come sit down and talk?"

Karen shook her head. "No. Especially not after what I just saw." She whirled on her heel and left the room.

I was not going to survive this. If my brother were guilty in any way of Lindsey's death, my relationship with my stepchildren — in particular, Karen — might be ruined forever.

Max leaned back on the couch.

I felt sick but needed to encourage him. "She's still insecure about losing her mother. That, on top of being a teenage girl."

He took a deep breath and stared at his hands; then he twirled his wedding ring around and around. "Maybe." He glanced at me. "Well, since we were interrupted anyway, what did you want to talk about?"

I wanted to tell him about Russ so badly, but the timing wasn't right. Besides, even though I might feel better for the confession, all I had was supposition. An accusation that may or may not be true. I had to know for certain.

"It can wait." I sat up straight. "You should go talk to Karen."

He frowned. "Are you sure?"

I nodded.

"I guess you're right." He kissed my cheek. "I'm really sorry, Trish."

"It's okay."

I watched him leave the room; then I followed more slowly, heading to our bedroom. It wasn't okay. I wondered if things would be okay ever again.

My mind whirled with the murder and accompanying complications.

Detective Scott hadn't given me any indication about the direction of the investigation, not that he would. I turned over all the possible suspects. Frank? His reaction at the scene didn't appear to be that of a guilty person, but what would I know about how guilty people acted? Though I had gone to school with him, I really didn't know Frank at all. His Dudley Do-It-All-Right reputation stood in place to this day. But that didn't mean Frank was a murderer. To the contrary, one could assume the opposite was the case.

Much of the staff of the store was sick that morning, at least according to Daryl. Besides the people at the registers up front, I'd only seen Lee Ann, Daryl, Frank, and a few customers. Who had the most to gain from Jim Bob's death? Besides me?

5

On Wednesday morning, I rushed through the front door of Four Oaks Self-Storage fifteen minutes late. I'd been sick that morning. I had to find out what was going on sooner rather than later so things could calm down, including my stomach.

Shirl peered over the high, gray Formica counter that surrounded her desk and held out some mail. "Hey, Mrs. C."

"Hi." I took the envelopes from her then went to my office where I fired up my computer and got to work. Max needed me to run through some figures for the new phase of construction across the street, as well as those for the new facility.

I heard the hum of cars arriving and leaving as customers came in to rent units or take care of bills. I paid no attention to anything until I heard the rumbling of Max's voice. He strolled into my office and shut the door. With his blue work shirt and jeans, he looked like every woman's dream of a hunky construction worker, with muscles in all the right places.

"Hi, honey." His gaze made me feel warm.

I leaned back in my chair. "Karen seemed okay this morning."

"Last night she accused me of acting like a teenage boy when I'm around you." He grinned, and his eyes sparkled, which made him look a lot like a teenager.

That could explain some of her hostile behavior. Not only was she jealous of me, she was also going through the stage where she didn't want to acknowledge that her father was a normal, healthy male. "You okay with that?" I asked.

He flashed me a wide smile. "What do you think?"

I motioned toward a chair. "You wanna sit?"

He shook his head. "Nope. I just came by to say hello. George is across the street at the site, checking out the work. Seeing him reminded me of you. He sends his regards."

I smiled at the mention of George's name. He'd introduced me to Max. "Tell him I said hi."

"Okay," Max said. "You remember the baseball game tonight, right?"

I nodded. The ball game might be a good

place to look for clues.

He walked around the desk and kissed me; then he headed for the front office. "I'll try to be home a bit early," he said over his shoulder. "That way we have time to eat dinner."

He left, banging the front door behind him. I went to the window to watch him cross the parking lot. The mention of George made me feel nostalgic. Even after six years, I still couldn't believe that I'd landed Max Cunningham. I clamped my fists tightly at my side. I would make sure that nothing happened to ruin what we had.

Time to gather clues. I walked out to the front office and leaned against the counter. Shirl was thumbing through a catalog.

"Can I talk to you?" I asked.

"Sure." She marked her place and faced me.

"What do you know about Jim Bob Jenkins?"

She crossed her arms. "Only that no one will miss the louse."

Well, that was straightforward and not a nice thing to say about a dead man. "Why is that?"

She shook her head. "He always acted like he was everyone's friend, but he was mean as a snake. Turn on a body faster than a rabid dog."

I nodded, and that encouraged her to continue.

"Then the old coot up and married that hussy. Nothin' good could come from that, I'll tell you what."

Louse, snake, mean dog, old coot — not a very flattering picture of the dearly departed. As for his wife, this was the second time I'd heard not-so-good things about her.

"Did you hear anything about suspects? Like Frank Gaines or Daryl Boyd?" I asked.

Shirl laughed. "Don't know much about Frank, but Daryl? That big weenie? Only way he'd kill someone is if he ran over 'em trying to get away from his wife when she's on a rampage."

I knew Daryl's wife and wouldn't blame anyone for running away from her.

"That's the thing, you know," Shirl said. "He married the woman for her money. She makes him work, so there he is at Shopper's Super Saver. He's too afraid of her to do anything. At least in front of her face." Shirl paused and tapped her finger on her forehead. "But you know what? Maybe Daryl is sneaky. You know how men can be when they want something."

I could only imagine what she meant by that comment, but she brought up a really good point. Sneakiness was an interesting character trait. Maybe it was just a short slide from being sneaky to slaughtering someone.

When I arrived home at noon, I saw a strange car parked out front on the road. An equally strange man stood on the sidewalk, looking at our house. I pulled my SUV into the driveway, and he turned around to peer at me.

I didn't get out, and I made sure I'd locked my doors. Finding Jim Bob's body had made me wary, more conscious of possible danger. Though we live in the country suburbs, we're near enough to larger towns to get the occasional roaming bad guy. The tall, skinny man, dressed in baggy chinos and a white knit shirt, ambled over to my car. I cracked the window and left my engine running, in case I had to make a quick getaway.

He said something to me, but I could barely hear him for staring at the massive gray and brown mop of hair that covered his head and his upper lip that sported the largest mustache I'd seen outside of Civil War movies.

"Mrs. Cunningham?"

"Who wants to know?" I demanded.

He flashed a smarmy, big-toothed smile. "I'm a reporter from the *Four Oaks Times Gazette.* Can you tell me about the body you found in the dairy case?"

I didn't want any more publicity over this whole thing. I didn't think Max or his parents would be happy, either.

"Look, Mr. . . ."

"Call me Carey." He paused. "Carey Snook." He reached out a hand, but I didn't roll down my window. He put his hand down. "Can you just tell me about the body you found in the dairy case?"

I shook my head. "No."

He shoved his hands in his pockets. "Is there another time I could come back, then?"

"No."

He stuck his face in my window. "You know, I want this story. Lots of people could be guilty of his murder. Everyone has secrets. That's what I'm looking for."

I couldn't speak. Was he implying something? What did he already know? He smiled and then turned, walked to his car, and hopped inside. I waited until he was out of sight before I parked my vehicle in the garage.

My legs felt shaky. All I needed was a newspaper person hounding me, looking for secrets. One more good reason to find my answers — fast.

I walked into the kitchen and flung my purse on the table as the phone rang.

I snatched the handset off the wall. "Hello?"

"Hello. Is Maxwell there?" A woman's voice, dripping a honeyed southern accent, came from the receiver.

"Maxwell?" Only Max's mother called him Maxwell. "Who's calling?"

"This is the Cunningham residence, isn't it?" For each syllable, she added another.

"Yes, but he's not available," I said. "Who is this?"

"He's not at work. I can't find him anywhere. Well, I guess I'll call him later then. Thank you."

She hung up without answering my question. I stood in the hall, holding my phone.

I'll be the first to admit I suffer from jealousy. Not because of anything Max has done. The way women respond to him isn't his fault. I just have a bit of a self-esteem problem. And right then, I felt even worse because I had this huge secret I was keeping from him.

So it was logical that I would wonder why a woman who wouldn't leave a message was looking all over the place for my husband. I wanted to ask him, but I couldn't reach him. I tried his cell phone, but he'd turned it off, which he sometimes does when he's in a meeting. Then I called the office only to have Shirl tell me that he was out and she didn't know where.

What to do? I paced the ceramic-tile floor in my kitchen waiting for Sammie to get home and trying to decide on my course of action. Knowing that Detective Scott was on the case made me edgy. I suspected I didn't have much time before he would discover that my altercation with Jim Bob was more than just what happened at the store. Now a hairy-faced reporter was sniffing around.

I had to think. Logically. This was no time to become unhinged. My first order of business was Russ. Had I really seen road signs in his closet? I took a deep breath and ticked off thoughts in my head. First, road signs. Second, find out who was talking to Jim Bob about Russ. One of Russ's old friends perhaps? For that I needed a list of who he'd known, and I knew just where to find one.

While my mother was at work and my father was away, Sammie and I could make a foray to the old family homestead and see if I could find a stop sign.

■ ■ ■ ■

"Mommy, what do you have to find here?" Sammie asked, as I pulled up to my parents'. The white Victorian farmhouse with its large, airy rooms and nooks and crannies had been my home from the time I was born until I moved into my own apartment. I missed living in an old house.

"I'm just getting something that Grandmom stored." I parked my vehicle next to the back porch. I'd told my mother that I needed to look for an old book. Not technically a lie, since I was going to get my brother's yearbooks, but I was disturbed that my half-truths were adding up. I undid Sammie's seat belt and mine, and we climbed out. Two white chickens scurried past us. Sammie laughed and began to chase them. "I'll be right back out," I yelled after her. "Stay in the yard."

I went in the back door, passed through a mudroom, and rushed into the kitchen. The smell of floor polish, lemon wax, and baking enveloped me, reminding me of coming home after school when I was little, grabbing a handful of cookies, and running outside to play. My biggest problem back then was escaping my mother's tongue. But now I was no longer a child. I was an adult with adult-sized problems.

I heard a dog bark and glanced out the window over the kitchen sink. Sammie was playing with Buddy, my father's border collie. Good. The dog was like a third parent. I hurried through the kitchen, down the hall to the staircase. I ran my hands over the smooth walnut handrail, thinking of all the times I'd slid down its length. The stairs, polished and worn from age, creaked under my feet as I jogged up them.

Russ's room was first on the right. Like all the other rooms, it was spacious, with dark wood trim and large, rectangular windows that reached almost from floor to ceiling. I went straight to his closet where I remembered seeing something covered with a sheet. Besides his clothes and shoes, there was very little. Russ was fanatically neat, a trait that would serve him well in the military. Had I imagined the sign?

I left his room and went down the hall to a door that led to the attic stairs. I scurried up those. At the top, I switched on a light and glanced around. Among my mother's many traits, good and bad, was compulsive organization. She labeled everything. I would have no problem finding his year-books. Each of us had plastic bins containing years of school paraphernalia.

I did a quick perimeter search, checking for road signs, as well. I was beginning to feel a sense of relief. Perhaps I hadn't seen a sign at all, and there was nothing to the threat. Maybe Jim Bob had made up the whole thing based on rumor, which I had to squelch.

"Mommy!" Sammie's voice came from the bottom of the stairs. "Can I come up?"

"No, honey. I'm coming down." I took another quick glance around with a lighter heart, opened Russ's high school box, and grabbed his yearbooks. Then I turned off the light and went down the stairs.

Sammie waited for me at the back door. "Buddy showed me where the new kittens are," she said. "In that old shed next to the garage. You wanna see?"

No, I didn't want to see. I'm not keen about cats even though I was raised with them, but I couldn't ignore Sammie's shining eyes.

"Okay, sweetie, show me."

My father built the small, clapboard lean-to next to the garage when I was Sammie's age. Years of white paint, lumpy in spots, covered the wood. He'd replaced the door recently with one that had a real handle instead of just a hook and eye. Sammie pointed to the corner where a tabby cat had made a bed with what looked to be an old insulated shirt of my dad's. Multicolored kittens, eyes barely opened, crawled over her.

I had to admit that the kittens were cute, but I wasn't looking at them. I was looking at the large, sheet-covered object behind them, feeling my heart fall to my toes.

6

My ride to the ball game with Max was subdued. Charlie and Sammie were home with Karen. Tommy was working. All I could think about was the stop sign I'd found in my father's shed.

Max didn't notice my preoccupation. He was telling me all about the meetings he'd had regarding the new self-storage facility. His typical male denseness was to my benefit tonight.

He parked the SUV at the community ball field. Another car whipped into the spot next to us. I grabbed my purse. Then I watched as a tall blond got out of the vehicle. She sashayed to the front of her car wearing a lime green skirt just this side of too short. A green-and-white-striped tank top showed off her other attributes, which the matching green sweater she had tied around her shoulders only partially covered. White, strappy, high-heeled sandals, not at all appropriate for a ball game, adorned her delicate feet.

When she saw us — in particular, Max — her eyes grew wide in her beautiful, oval face. Then she smiled and waved as if greeting an old friend.

I surmised from the woman's reaction that she knew my husband. When I turned on Max, I had only one question. "Who is that?"

"Stefanie Jenkins," Max said, undoing his seat belt.

"Who?" The name sounded familiar.

"Jim Bob's wife, er, widow," he said.

The widow sidled over to my husband's window. He opened it.

"Maxwell?" I heard her southern accent and knew I'd spoken with her earlier that day. "May I speak with you?"

"Shouldn't she be grieving at home?" I whispered in Max's ear, as suspicion niggled in my brain.

He smiled at her. "I'll be out in just a moment." He put the window up and turned to face me. "Trish, be nice. She just lost her husband."

"Exactly my point." I jammed my index finger into his shoulder for emphasis. "Shouldn't she be grieving at home?"

"Let's go, baby." He kissed me thoroughly.

"I've got to get our team settled."

He was out of the car first and joined Stefanie, who leaned too close to him for my liking. I joined them quickly, and she greeted me with a white, toothy smile.

"You must be Trish. Maxwell speaks so highly of you." She looked down at me with those wide baby blues. "I'm Stefanie with an *F.* You can call me Steffie."

"Steffie." I nodded. It sounded so collegiate. I looked closer at the widow. No wrinkles. No mustache hairs. She even looked collegiate. Now I understood why my mother had oozed disapproval over Jim Bob's marriage, and why, if such a thing were possible, Estelle would have turned over in her grave.

"I'm so sorry for your loss," I said, watching her and wondering why she was here.

As if she read my thoughts, tears welled up in her eyes. "Thank you. And I want to express my sympathy that you were the unfortunate one to . . . find . . . my husband."

I'd seen better acting on Saturday-morning cartoons. Something about her wasn't right, which explained why I said what I said next.

"I'm really surprised that you're out and about so soon. Especially to a ball game."

Max looked down at me in surprise; then he put his arm around my shoulders and squeezed. I put my arm around his waist and pinched him in return as I smiled sweetly at Stefanie.

Tears hung on her eyelashes. She blinked rapidly, and I couldn't tell if she was fluttering her eyelids or getting rid of tears. "I just couldn't sit at home by myself. I heard about the game and decided it would be a distraction for me."

"It's a good idea," Max the Dense said.

She turned to him and batted her eyes.

An older couple I knew from church arrived and offered their sympathies to her. Max took my hand and led me to the other side of my SUV. Concern wrinkled his forehead. "Trish, I can't remember your ever being so unkind. Well, except around my mother, which is understandable. What's wrong?"

I stared up at him while I tried to figure out just exactly what was bothering me besides a raging attack of jealousy. "Stefanie called you today at our house, but she wouldn't leave a message. She said she'd been looking all over for you and couldn't find you."

"What?" He frowned at me.

"I know it was her. Who can miss that accent?"

"Honey . . ."

"There's something not right with her, Max. I mean, her husband just died. She's never come to a ball game before — I would have noticed. And as far as I know, she doesn't know any of the players. Besides, I don't like the way she looks at you."

"People sometimes do strange things when someone they know dies," he said.

"Not her. She's up to no good." I meant that in more ways than one.

"Are you jealous?" he asked.

I put my hands on my hips. "Should I be?"

He laughed. "I'm flattered, but you've got a really suspicious mind. You should work with Eric Scott."

That gave me pause.

Max must have seen my expression. "Hey, I'm not serious. I want you to leave all that behind you." He grabbed my hand and squeezed it. "You have nothing to worry about, by the way. I adore you."

He didn't understand at all.

An hour later, I sat at the top of the hard, metal bleachers. A cool breeze blew, and I was glad I'd worn long sleeves. I glanced around at the crowd and noticed Stefanie seated at ground level next to the same couple who had spoken with her earlier.

As I contemplated the widow's pert nose and perfect hair, I realized that Max hadn't told me how he knew her. That aggravated me, so I went to the soda machine to get something to drink. While I stood there deciding, April May Winters, one of my mother's employees, wandered up.

"Hey, Trish." The chubby redhead contemplated sodas over my shoulder.

"Hi, April."

"I see Miss Priss Stefanie Jenkins is here."

Ah, perhaps here would be a source of information. I hastily picked a Diet Coke, pushed the button, and then pulled out more quarters. "You want a soda?"

"Well, sure," she said enthusiastically. "Grape."

I put more money into the machine and out popped the soda, which I handed to her. I watched her open it and take a huge gulp.

"Stefanie told me and Max that she's so sad and lonely she's come here for company," I said.

April May choked. I thought I might have to do the Heimlich maneuver, but she recovered. "She said that? I can't believe it. She must think you guys are stupid or something."

That's not exactly what I wanted to hear.

My mouth must have been hanging open because April immediately backtracked.

"Oh, sorry. That sounded really bad. I didn't mean it. I don't think you and Max are dumb."

"It's okay. We might be a little stupid when it comes to Stefanie." I said *we* when I really meant *he,* but April didn't have to know that. "So Stefanie's not grieving?" I asked.

April snorted about ten times, which is the way she laughs, and I worried that she would choke again. When she regained control, she shook her head. "She married the man for his money. Unfortunately, Jim Bob was as sneaky as he was ugly and mean, er . . . God rest his soul."

Now I had two sneaky men for my list. And April was the third person I'd spoken to who had nothing good to say about Jim Bob. "He had money? Why was he a pharmacist?"

"Dunno." She shrugged. "I just heard he had it, but he didn't act like it, nasty tightwad. He made your mother deliver a box of free doughnuts to the pharmacy once a week."

That was news to me, but I didn't have time to think about it because April was on a roll.

"Him and Miss Fancy-Pants met out

there on one of them Cayman Islands. You know, like what you hear about? Where people swim buck naked and all. I mean, imagine." She paused, possibly to do just that.

I didn't know anything about the Caymans or swimming nude and didn't care, but I nodded anyway. She took my attention very seriously. I doubted she had much opportunity to talk when she worked with my mother.

"Well, next thing you know, here he comes back to Four Oaks married to her. Everyone knew what she was up to. I mean, her and him? The old goat." Snort. "He must have been really stupid. Of course, he is a man." She snorted three more times.

I'm not a man basher, but tonight I was irritated enough with my husband's lack of astuteness about Stefanie to agree. I smiled widely and nodded again to encourage April to continue.

"Well, they lived in unhappiness. Can't figure out why they stayed together."

"Hey, April!" someone shouted from the bleachers.

"Gotta go," she said. "It's been good to talk. You know, I don't always agree with your mother."

Neither do I, but I wondered which of my

mother's opinions about me April referred to. She walked away, and my head spun. Too much information in too short a time. With April May's comments, my temper had subsided, and I felt compelled to go back to the game and support Max. On rare occasions, he stopped thinking about the team's performance long enough to look for me in the bleachers for a thumbs-up. I needed to be there just in case. Besides, watching him play is a pleasure all its own.

Max's team won, which didn't surprise me. The intrepid Detective Scott played almost as well as Max. I wandered around, shooting the breeze with people, watching Stefanie out of the corner of my eye. She had a lot of hair. A long, bleached-blond, curly pouf, resembling what I'd seen on beauty contestants. She met my eye and tottered over to me on her high heels. Without being rude, there was no way I could avoid her.

"Oh, Trish. The game was wonderful. Max is so talented. He plays like a pro."

"Thanks," I murmured. I hoped his game was his only quality she'd been watching.

I was so busy fighting my bad feelings that I didn't see Detective Eric Scott until he was standing next to me.

He smiled. I thought I would fall over.

"Hello, Trish." He turned his gaze on Steffie. "Mrs. Jenkins. How are you tonight?"

She focused her big baby blues on him. "Oh, Detective Scott. You are such a good ball player."

"Thank you." He continued to smile, but I saw past that to his eyes. Shrewd and assessing. I was relieved that he wasn't looking at me for once. "It's a team effort, of course," he said. "No one person is responsible for our game."

She blinked several times and continued to smile brightly. "Oh, that is so true." She turned to me. "Maxwell is so good."

If she said one more thing about how good Max was, I was going to hit her.

"Must be hard to be out so soon after the death of Jim Bob," Detective Scott said.

I coughed trying to cover a laugh. I was thinking better and better of him.

"This is such a good distraction for me." Tears filled her eyes again. "Detective Scott, I'm so impressed by your dedication to finding the person who did this."

As far as I was concerned, she was laying it on a little thick.

"Have no fear, Mrs. Jenkins; I'll solve this crime." He jauntily saluted us. "Ladies. I have to get a move on. Crime fighting never ends." He jogged away. As I watched him go, I noticed a bald man disappear behind the cement building that held the bathrooms. I didn't recognize him.

Stefanie sighed. I turned back to her.

"Seeing the police brings back my loss," she said in a breathy voice. "I need to go home."

She walked in the direction of the parking lot. I wandered around the grounds, greeting people. Peggy Nichols, the principal of Charlie and Sammie's school, stopped me. "Trish, will you still be able to man your booth this Saturday?" She squinted at me through thick glasses.

"Sure. I'm fine."

She shook her head. "I wouldn't be if I were you. I can't believe all the things happening in our little town. It's like a bacteria eating from the inside out."

That was certainly descriptive. Unfortunately, it sounded a little like what was happening to me. I was being eaten up inside by guilt. We chatted a bit more; then I left to find Max and noticed Stefanie coming from the bathroom. That was strange. I thought she'd been in a hurry to leave.

7

When Max and I returned home, Karen was passing through the foyer on her way to her room with the cordless. In the past, when I'd suggested she have one permanently implanted, she wasn't amused. But then what did I expect? When she turned fifteen, she lost her sense of humor and ceased to be amused by anything I said.

Max motioned for her to wait.

She sighed hugely and put her hand over the receiver. "What, Dad? This is really important. Julie is afraid her mother has a boyfriend. He's a loser who works at some school. Julie's crying. She wants her dad."

Lee Ann dating someone else? She and Norm had been together since high school — inseparable. He'd rescued her from an abusive home situation. I still couldn't imagine their breaking up.

"Were there any phone calls for us?" Max asked.

She shook her head. "Nah. No phone calls except Grandmom. Oh, and Abbie called to say she'd pick up doughnuts for the health fair."

Those weren't considered real phone calls, since they weren't for Karen.

She tapped her fingers on the railing. "Sammie's in bed and wants you to come up and hug her good night. Charlie's in his room. He keeps talking about dead people." She sighed and rolled her eyes toward the ceiling. "Why do I have to have such a weird brother? Why do I have such a weird family?" She put the phone back to her mouth and tromped up the stairs.

Max and I exchanged glances.

"I think I'll talk to Charlie tonight about the dead people after I tuck Sammie in and pray with her."

"Okay," he said. "But I don't think it's any big deal. He's probably just teasing the girls. You know how he is."

I did, perhaps better than Max. Charlie and I are like soul mates. We feel deeply, have great imaginations, and we're both scrappers.

I went upstairs to say good night to Sammie, but I was too late. She was already asleep. I stood next to her canopy bed and watched as hair that had fallen over her face rose and fell with her breaths. My baby. I was praying for her when Max joined me. He stood quietly next to me until I was done.

When we were back in the hall, he headed for the stairs. "I'll be in my office," he said over his shoulder. "I have to call George. Remember, he'll be in tomorrow morning to talk about the figures you put together. Since you know all the details, you can explain them to him."

"Okay." I watched him go downstairs and wished we could have one day with no one around and nothing between us.

I peeked into Charlie's room. His wiry, pajama-clad body was huddled in a chair at his desk where he intently studied an open book.

"You ready for bed?" I asked.

He jumped as if I'd set off a firecracker. "Uh, yeah." He slammed the book shut and shoved it under his schoolbooks.

Nothing says guilty like a child hiding something from his parent's view. "What is that, Charlie?"

He stared at me defiantly. "It's just a book."

"What book?" I walked over to his desk.

He heaved a sigh and pulled it back out from under the pile with exaggerated motions. "Here."

Mysterious Disappearances — The Facts, Plain and Simple.

Okay, well, at least it wasn't a book of naked women. Still, the way he hid it told me he knew what I'd say about it.

"So they put out a book?" I fingered the cover, illustrated by superimposed, graphic, black-and-white crime images. "Whose is this?"

"Mike's."

I didn't know how to handle this situation. "I told you I don't like that show."

He stared at the floor. "I know."

I ruffled his hair. "Sweetie, is this what makes you see ghosts?"

His head shot up. "What are you talking about?"

"You don't see ghosts?"

His disapproving frown was similar to Max's. "Mom, I don't believe in stuff like that."

"But Karen said something about it," I said.

Charlie snorted. "Karen. She's a girl."

"And that means?"

"Well, all she does is talk on the phone with Julie. She needs a life. She needs to stop listening to other people and make up her own mind about things."

Okay, then. I guess that settled that. Perhaps Max was right, and Charlie was just teasing his sisters. "Well, why don't you return the book to Mike tomorrow? We'll just drop the whole thing."

Charlie stared at me. I could tell he was trying to find a loophole, but he finally nodded. "Okay."

I wanted to smile, but I didn't. He was so much like me he could have been my biological son.

After we prayed together, I tucked Charlie into bed; then I sat down in front of the television and flipped to the local news.

The perky news anchor read a teaser about the local landfill, which was temporarily closing. That's where Norm, Lee Ann's husband, worked.

The newscaster moved on to the murder at the grocery store. "The local Shopper's Super Saver is now open after the body of pharmacist Jim Bob Jenkins, a local resident, was discovered murdered in the refrigerated room behind the dairy case. Police report that the investigation is ongoing. A source close to the situation has indicated that store finances might be involved. Store manager Frank Gaines spoke with us earlier."

They cut to a clip of an interview with

poor Frank. His charming, Dudley Do-It-All-Right persona had lost quite a bit of its shine. His hair was flat, and his tie was crooked.

The newsperson shoved the mike closer into Frank's face. "Can you tell us what you know about the murder investigation?"

If I were a betting person, I would wager that Frank's scowl indicated more than minor irritation. "I'm not privy to the investigation," he snarled. "I have nothing to say."

Yep. I was right.

The news cut back to the studio. Ms. Perky beamed into the camera, as though she'd just covered a cheery piece of Americana. Then she babbled on about an investigation at the landfill — something about hauling in medical waste from New Jersey.

I turned off the television. The phone rang. Why would someone call this late? Shortly after, I heard Tommy tromping down the stairs.

"Where's Dad? He's got a call." He waved the phone in the air.

"In his study," I said. "Who is it?"

He covered the receiver. "It's Mrs. Jenkins."

Dear Steffie. Now why was she calling Max? I jumped up from the couch. "Give me the phone. I'll take it to your father." I snatched it from Tommy's hand.

He stared at me with an open mouth. "Mom, Dad has a phone in his office, you know."

"Yes, I know."

I trotted down the hall, pushed open the study door, and marched inside.

"Come on in," Max said, staring at me over reading glasses, with a slight grin on his lips. His desk was littered with bluish architectural plans.

I made sure my hand was over the receiver. "The phone's for you. It's Steffie." I said it as if it were a four-letter word.

Max took off his glasses, pinched the bridge of his nose, and then picked up the phone on his desk.

Okay, so I have no pride. I listened in on the headset I held.

"Maxwell, hello." At least six syllables.

"Hello, Stefanie." He glanced at me.

"I'm so sorry to call you so late. I hope I didn't wake your wife." Did Steffie want to talk to Max without my knowing? My grip on the phone got tighter.

"No, it's fine," Max said. "What can I do for you?"

I sat in a chair opposite his desk. He

looked up at me with a slight grin and winked.

Stefanie began to talk. "Sugar, I need to get into Jim Bob's unit as soon as possible. There are things in there I absolutely must have."

Sugar? I raised my eyebrows and watched Max.

"I told you that I need a court order." He spoke in a low, even tone and tapped his fingers on the desk.

My mind processed the information. Jim Bob must have had a storage unit contract on which Steffie's name wasn't listed.

"But surely you can understand given my delicate state that I can't wait for those old judges to make a decision. Please, sugar, make this teeny little exception for me."

I stuck my finger into my mouth and pretended to gag.

Max ignored me. He also ignored her pleas. "I'm sorry. I can't make any exceptions."

I stared at him in admiration. There is something terribly attractive about a man who can say something like that and still sound nice. In the silence that followed, I heard her breathing. I wondered if she was going to offer a bribe of the intimate sort to get the unit open, in which case I would be obligated to find her and rip out her hair.

"Please, Maxwell. Just take me into the unit. You can stand there. I only need a couple teeny little papers. Nothing big. I'll make it worth your while."

"Worth your while" was open to interpretation. Unfortunately, it wasn't blatant enough to excuse any ripping or tearing. Max met my gaze and tapped his fingers harder on the desk. "I'm sorry, Stefanie. I have to obey the law."

The Widow Jenkins's sweetness slipped. "This is an inconvenience, you know."

Max stayed right on the party line. "I understand you're inconvenienced. I want to open it for you and will as soon as I can."

She sniffed. "I guess that will have to do."

"I'm sorry," Max said. "If there's anything else we can do for you, please let us know."

I hung up after he did and put my phone on the floor. He stared at me with a smirk on his lips.

I hopped up, walked over to him with exaggerated swings of my hips, and leaned against the edge of his desk in my best imitation of a femme fatale. "Sugar, just do what I want, and I'll make it worth your while." My imitation sounded surprisingly like her.

Max grinned and pulled me close. "You

really dislike Steffie."

I ran my finger over his lips. "Dislike? No. It's nothing personal. I just don't like her going on and on about how good you are. Besides, I have a bad feeling about her."

He had the nerve to laugh. "You're adorable."

"Chauvinist," I said.

"Guilty as charged." Max pulled me into his lap. "You have nothing to worry about. And I guess you figured out what's going on. She's even been by the office a couple of times. She needs to get into a storage unit that Jim Bob rented a year ago, but her name isn't on the contract."

"I guess we can't, either, can we?" I glanced at him hopefully, wishing we could take one little look.

Max kissed me lightly. "Curious, aren't you? But you're right. I won't touch it at this point until everything is settled. It's just too bad people don't think about things like emergency access in case of injury or death when they rent units."

Of all the negative character traits I'd heard about Jim Bob, stupidity wasn't one of them. I wondered if he'd left Stefanie off the contract on purpose.

8

"You're going to call the doctor today, right?" Max asked as he buttoned his shirt in the mirror.

"I'll be fine, Max." I had spent the first few minutes out of bed that morning being sick. Now I was trying to figure out what to wear.

He turned around to face me and gave me a once-over. "Trish, you haven't been feeling well for days."

I finally decided on nice jeans and a pink shirt. "I'm just overwrought. It's got to be nerves. Stop worrying." Of course, that's what happens when you keep secrets and guilt eats you from the inside out. I yanked on the shirt.

He blinked, and his mouth twitched. "Touchy, aren't you?"

"Well, I'm just tired of everyone telling me that I don't look well. It makes me feel flabby and white, like my mother's doughnut dough." I adjusted my blouse collar and glared at him. "So stop thinking that."

He grinned. "I wasn't thinking that."

I put my hands on my hips. "Well, then, what were you thinking?"

He walked around the bed. "Actually, I was reflecting on how good you look."

"What?"

His eyes had that little gleam in them.

"Max, we have a meeting and —"

I can't talk and kiss. And once again, my guilty conscience was bugging me, which was distressing because kissing Max is one of the joys of my life. However, pounding at our bedroom door distracted both of us.

"Mom!" Charlie shouted. "I can't find my math book."

Interruption by child. Morning had begun.

Doughnuts were in my blood. Hopefully the fat wasn't. My mother began perfecting her doughnut recipes when I was too little to eat them. Now she owned Doris's Doughnuts. The store was in a tiny strip mall near Four Oaks Self-Storage, so I decided to stop by and pick up a dozen to take for the guys in the meeting. George, the contractor who would be in the office this morning, loved my mother's doughnuts.

Since she now offers a lunch menu as well as baked goods and coffee that rival the chains, the store is a favorite spot for everyone from construction workers to cops. I sincerely hoped there would be no cops there today.

The bell above my head rang as I walked into the bright red and white room. The scent of coffee and fresh doughnuts made my mouth water. Ma looked up from behind the cash register. From the glance she gave me, I knew I was in for it.

"Well, it's about time." No one's voice is louder than my mother's, especially when she's trying to make a point. Everyone in the place looked up. "People have been asking about my daughter. I say, what daughter?"

"Oh, sure. I never talk to you. I'm surprised you even recognize me." I headed for the self-serve coffee, recalling what the pastor had told me in premarital counseling about one of the sources of my self-esteem issues — my mother.

"Just like kids, isn't it?" Gail, my mother's best friend and longtime help, nodded like a bobblehead doll. "Ungrateful. All of them. We give birth, go through all that agony, and then what?"

As if I hadn't gone through labor myself. I

ignored them and poured some fresh Colombian into a Styrofoam cup at the self-serve counter. Then I scoped out the fresh, doughy, fattening circles.

"One day you'll wish you had visited me every day," Ma said as she handed a customer a bag stuffed with pastry. "When I'm dead and gone, buried next to your father."

"Yeah, yeah, whatever," I said under my breath. She was on a roll. The white tables and chairs were mostly filled, which meant she had an audience for her comments — something she reveled in. I tried not to take her seriously, but dealing with her barbs was hard.

"Are you here to buy?" she asked.

I took a huge sip of coffee. "Yeah. I need a dozen to take to work. You choose. Oh, and a bear claw, too. That's my breakfast."

"Something going on?" She deftly picked up the doughnuts and boxed them.

"A meeting with George about the expansion." The coffee wasn't settling well in my stomach.

"I'm surprised you can eat anything after finding poor Jim Bob stabbed to death, sprawled over a grocery cart, guts in all directions," Gail said as she turned on the espresso machine. "It's only been four days."

Well, there went my appetite.

"I mean, really, imagine the blood," she continued as steam hissed from the machine and brown liquid squirted into a tiny cup.

Ma sadly shook her head in total agreement. "What a mess. I wonder if they hired someone to clean up the floor."

My stomach twisted.

April May came from the back with flour on her hands. "I heard there was gore from one end of that place to another."

Ma looked at April and back at Gail. "Now, do you suppose there are companies that do that sort of thing? Clean up murder scenes? Can you imagine? What happens to all the parts?"

The memory of Jim Bob came back with a vengeance. The coffee in my stomach curdled. "Back in a minute," I managed to gasp as I slapped my hand over my mouth. I made it to the bathroom just in time. When I'd finished, I pulled a cleaning wipe from a plastic pouch in my purse and wiped my mouth. I stood for a few minutes in the bathroom, waiting for my stomach to settle. After I stuck a piece of gum in my mouth, I went back to the counter.

"Are you sick?" Ma asked.

"I think I have a bug or something." I was beginning to suspect I was allergic to caffeine or had an ulcer. I paid for my coffee and the doughnuts, although it would be awhile before I could ingest either.

"I hope you're not pregnant," she said in a loud voice.

From the sudden silence and surreptitious looks from the people sitting at tables, everyone in the room heard her. Great. Now rumors would fly. I felt heat crawl up my face. There was no way I could be pregnant. The doctors said so. Sammie had been a miracle.

"That's all you need — more kids. Four is plenty," she said as the bobbleheads Gail and April nodded rapidly in the background. "You don't want to be like all them Perrys havin' all those kids out in their shantytown near the landfill." She took a deep breath.

"I can't imagine how they do it," Gail chimed in. "I mean Cheryl Perry must have one every nine months."

I considered explaining exactly how it was done, but I refrained.

"Landfill germs," my mother said. "They breathe 'em in every day, especially now."

April May wrapped a breakfast sandwich in foil for a customer. "Think of the hospital bills."

"That's probably why doctors cost so

much," Gail said. "I mean, even with insurance we're robbed blind. Look at all I just paid when I was there the other day."

"I spent years paying off my three children," my mother said, eyeing me as if I were responsible for me and my brothers.

"Nowadays, people like the Perrys don't have to pay for nothing." Gail slapped a coffee-filter basket against the edge of a trash can, and the used filter slid into its depths. "The government pays for everything out of our pockets. Bunch of thieves."

"Well, some people just don't have good insurance," April said, the voice of reason.

"Then they should get jobs," Gail pontificated. "I mean, even Shopper's Super Saver has good insurance. I overheard what Daryl's co-pay was that day I went. And he had stitches and a smashed finger."

Before the conversation digressed further, I decided to leave. I waved at my mother, but before I stepped out the door, I heard Dudley Do-It-All-Right's name and halted midstep.

"And what's going to happen to Shopper's Super Saver now after all that stuff about Frank is out in the open?" Gail clucked her tongue.

I turned back around to listen.

"You can't be too careful these days. The

best people can be living double lives," April May intoned.

"Isn't that the truth?" Gail looked up at me as if I were hiding the very worst of secrets, which I was.

Ma nodded. "Just look at Frank. He's always been perfect. His wife, kids, and house are perfect. Those two youngest of his are cute as bugs. They go to Sammie and Charlie's school, you know."

"That just goes to show you," Gail said.

I waited to find out what it goes to show, but no one said anything.

"What do you think he did with the money?" Ma asked.

Gail put on a new pot of coffee. "Gold. I'm sure he bought gold." She's convinced that the world is headed for a financial collapse and gold is the only safe investment. She also believes that NASA faked the moonwalk.

They busied themselves behind the counter. I waited. My mother finally looked at me, hands on her hips.

"You need something else? You should sit down if you don't feel well. You certainly look like it. Something about your face. Pasty and a little swollen like you're holding water maybe? Is your blood pressure okay?"

I reached up to feel my face, expecting it

to feel spongy, like a balloon. If I hadn't felt bad before, I did now. "I should go," I said.

"Well, don't let me stop you. At least I'll see you again on Sunday."

My mind was whirling, but not because of Sunday dinner. "Before I go, I want to know about Frank," I said.

Gail almost dropped the mug she held. "You mean you don't know?"

April stared at me openmouthed. "I would have thought you'd know everything seeing as how you're in the loop and so close to the police and all."

"Rumors 'R Us" had been busy. Of course, this was their company headquarters. But why did April think I was in the know with Detective Eric Scott?

"Where in the world did you get that idea?" I asked.

"Your mother's been telling everyone about it," April May said. "You've been called in for meetings a couple of times."

I stared at my mother in disbelief. She'd always done that. Made me feel like a loser in private but bragged to everyone about all my accomplishments — even those I hadn't done. She lived in a different reality. I was a suspect, for crying out loud. But there was no sense in trying to convince the bobble-heads. They'd believe what she wanted them to believe. "Just tell me about Frank, please."

Gail, April, and Ma exchanged glances.

She sighed. "Frank has been stealing money from the store."

Frank? Dudley Do-It-All-Right? Stealing from the store? "Embezzling?" I asked.

"See," Ma said triumphantly. "You knew. You just wanted to see if we knew."

I headed for the door once again. "See you later, Ma."

She waved her hand in the air, and I left. In my SUV, I placed the box of doughnuts on the passenger seat, musing how easy it was to think you really knew someone when, in reality, you didn't know them at all. Of all the people in town, I would never, ever have thought Frank capable of embezzling.

This was an interesting turn of events. Did Frank's crime have anything to do with Jim Bob's death? I pulled a pen from my purse and turned over the receipt my mother had given me to jot some notes. Using the dashboard like a desk, I started to write. *Embezzling. Frank a murderer?*

Gail had said something . . . something that was important. I was so engrossed in my thoughts I didn't see Detective Eric Scott until he tapped on my window. I jumped and stuffed the paper and pen into my purse. He motioned for me to roll down the glass. As I did, Corporal Nick Fletcher, otherwise known as Santa Cop, nodded at me from an unmarked car. Stupid me. I'd stayed too long.

I looked up at the tall, blond detective. "Are you harassing me?"

"I hope not," he said in a mild tone.

"Then why won't you leave me alone? I see you all the time now." I glanced at the window of my mother's store. She, Gail, and April were watching us. That was maddening, and I turned on him. "Do you realize that everyone thinks I'm in some sort of inner circle with you? My mother is convinced that I'm like your confidante or something because you've hauled me in to the sheriff's office twice now. They won't believe I'm just another suspect. And this is not going to help. Not at all."

He glanced at the store then back at me. "I'm sorry. No one is accusing you of anything."

There was that mild, even tone again. "Detective Scott, are you trained to sound nice even when you don't want to? Is it how you get people to talk to you?"

The left side of his mouth lifted. A half

smile that told me everything I needed to know.

I sighed. "I have to go to work. What do you want?"

"I was going to suggest that perhaps we need to have another talk."

My heart pounded. "Why?"

"Just to see if you remember anything else." He shifted. The gold circle–enclosed star glittered on his belt in the early morning sun; then I noticed a serious-looking black gun nestled in a brown leather holster at his side.

I glanced up and met his gaze. "Do I have to?"

He leaned his upper arm on the hood of my SUV and stared down at me. "Might be a good thing."

I felt claustrophobic with him hovering over me like that. "Well —"

"How about this afternoon? Say around two?"

"I have to find someone to watch Sammie." I mentally went through a list in my head. Then I looked up at him. "If I come in to talk to you, will you do me a favor?"

He straightened and narrowed his eyes. "I don't work like that."

"Please. It's nothing bad." I glanced at the store where Gail had her face pressed against the glass. Her mouth was moving rapidly. I could only imagine what she was saying. "Could you tell my mother that you and I aren't working together? Maybe she'll believe you."

He glanced from me to the store and back to me. Then he laughed. "I come here almost every morning, and I have for years. I know your mother well enough to say with confidence that no one can deter her from anything she thinks."

There we had it from a police detective — what I'd known my whole life.

After watching the three aforementioned women watch Detective Scott and Corporal Fletcher enter the store, I slumped in my seat. Another interview. And I hadn't had time to find out what I needed to know. If I could just come up with an idea before I met with the detective, then maybe I could distract him. What had Gail said? Something about the murder scene? Now that my stomach had gone back to normal, I could picture everything in my mind without throwing up. What was it that bugged me? There was Jim Bob on a cart and a nasty-looking knife in his chest and . . . no blood. That's what was wrong. How could Jim Bob have been stabbed to death without blood going all over? Perhaps I missed it all. A trick of my mind to protect me. Still, I wasn't sure, and that bothered me.

George and I were sitting in my office after the meeting, eating doughnuts while Max ran a few errands. Years ago, when I worked for George as his office manager, we got doughnuts once a week and sat together just like this. In fact, it was over doughnuts when he'd first introduced me to Max, who had been inquiring about George's contracting business.

I swallowed a bite of my bear claw. "Did you know Jim Bob Jenkins?"

He frowned and wiped his mouth on a napkin. "Enough to know he was a . . . Well, I don't want to use that kind of language in front of you, Trish."

"Can't you tell me without cussing?" I took another bite.

He shook his head. "Not sure I can, and I hate to speak ill of the dead."

"No one else hesitates," I said through crumbs on my lips.

He smiled. "I'm sure they don't. He didn't exactly inspire good feelings in folks."

I waited.

George eyed me. "You got a reason for asking?"

"Curiosity. I found the body."

"Yes, well, that was too bad. No woman should see something like that. Max is worried about you. Says the whole thing might have given you an ulcer."

"Max worries too much." I sniffed and wiped my fingers.

George grinned at me. "For good reason, besides which he's nuts over you. Was from the first time he saw you."

I grinned back, happy with the thought that Max was nuts for me; then I remembered that maybe the only reason I had Max was because my brother killed Lindsey.

George misinterpreted my change of expression. "Okay, I'll tell you. You don't need to get upset." The chair squeaked under his weight as he crossed his legs. "Jim Bob was always trying to find people's weak spots. He'd make like he was so nice. Then idiots would confide stuff, or somebody would tell him something about somebody else, and he'd use it to get things from them. He tried it with me. I told him to . . . er, stop it."

That sounded suspiciously like what Jim Bob had done to me. "You mean blackmail?"

"You could call it that," George said.

"Doesn't sound like he was a nice guy at all." I frowned at him. "If he was blackmailing people, why didn't someone tell the police?"

George shook his head. "Lack of proof, for one thing. And the other reason was that people probably didn't want their dirty little secrets to get out."

I stared at the napkin in my lap. Dirty little secrets. That added a real dimension to motivation for his death. Apparently I was only one of many who had motivation to kill Jim Bob. I wondered if Steffie knew about her husband's activities. I looked up at George. "What do you think of Stefanie?"

"Her?" His guttural tone made the pronoun sound like a bad word. "All's I can say is they deserved each other."

"So you don't think she's attractive?" I couldn't help it. I had to know.

He snorted. "Please, Trish. I'm too old to have my head turned by a pretty face. Yeah, she's got some obvious, er, attributes, but there's different kinds of pretty. You got what'll last. You're a fine-looking, nice, interesting young woman."

Max sauntered into the office with his arms behind his back. "Are you flirting with my wife, George?"

He laughed. "I'm too old, buddy. Couldn't keep up with her if I had to. That kind of spunk needs someone who can handle it.

Like you."

I blushed.

Max regarded me with a smoky glance that made my blood warm. Then he took his hands from behind his back. He held a bouquet of flowers. Roses.

"For you, baby," he said and smiled. "Having George around is bringing back lots of good memories."

George grinned. "See? He's nuts over you."

I stood and took the flowers from Max, blinking back tears. He leaned over and kissed my forehead. "I love you," he whispered. "George is right."

"Thank you, honey." I buried my face in the blooms so he wouldn't see just how upset I was. I didn't deserve flowers. Not at all.

Max slipped into a chair, stretching his legs out, crossing them at the ankles. "Honey, you remember that self-storage convention in Chicago?"

I nodded, glad for the change of topic. After I put the flowers on my desk, I took a deep breath and sat down. The family had gone a few years ago when Max and his dad first started planning their self-storage empire.

"It's coming up in couple of days," he said.

I nodded again.

He watched me. "Getting the kids taken care of, like their car pools and things, is hard with short notice."

"That's true," I murmured. Still, the thought of time away from here was wonderful. We'd have time alone together. We could really talk, and then, far away from the familiar, I could tell Max everything. I began making a mental list of phone calls I would make if we went.

"You should go," George said. "You gotta get things settled. With plans in the works for the new facility, you gotta get some good programs. Nothin' chases the renters away like not being able to get into their units or keeping their stuff in a facility that isn't secured."

Our gate program still wasn't working right, and we had to leave the gate open twenty-four hours — something that we had to take care of soon.

I glanced at my watch. Time had gotten away from me. I jumped to my feet. "I have to go. I have to find someone to watch Sammie. I, ah, have to go see Detective Scott this afternoon."

"Again?" Max frowned. "This is the third time. Why?"

I shrugged. "He has a few more questions.

It's just standard procedure."

"I wouldn't think so . . . unless you're a suspect." He frowned. "Are you? Eric didn't say anything last night, but you were at the store, and you did find the body." He paused. "Honey, is there something you're not telling me?"

I tried not to choke.

George cleared his throat and stood. "I think it's time for me to head out."

Max was distracted for a moment, saying good-bye to George. That meant I had just a second's reprieve. My husband might be dense to certain subtleties of mood, but once he latched onto something, his mind was like lightning — and he didn't let go until he had answers. I needed to figure things out quickly. Perhaps Max would pick up Sammie, and I'd have time for a quick visit to Abbie's.

I turned to my desk and picked up my flowers as the guys said their good-byes. Maybe I could distract him.

"Trish?"

I stuck my nose in the flowers. "Where did you get these? They're lovely."

"Glad you like them." I felt his eyes boring into the back of my head.

I reached for my purse. "Would you pick up Sammie for me, honey? I might like to visit Abbie before I go to the sheriff's office."

"No problem," he said softly.

I made sure my phone was in my purse. "I'll pick up something from the deli for dinner, okay? How about subs? And a movie? We can watch a movie tonight."

He cleared his throat.

I slowly turned around. Max had his arms crossed.

"I should go now," I said.

"I think you should tell me what's going on first." The only part of him that moved was his mouth. His eyes were slightly narrowed, and he looked a bit like a panther ready to pounce. I rarely saw Max's aggressive side. A hard-nosed businessman who had learned at the feet of his harder-nosed father. I didn't like it.

I clasped the handle of my purse until my knuckles turned white. "Detective Scott says that by talking to me over and over again, things I've seen but don't remember might come back to me." As much as the detective had annoyed me, I couldn't believe I was defending him.

Max studied me very much like the cops had. Then he took a deep breath and glanced at his watch. "Something's not right here, but I need to go pick up Sammie. This is the last time I'll allow you to go to the sheriff's office without a lawyer. I want you to tell Eric that, okay?"

Great. All I needed was a lawyer friend of the Cunninghams picking my brain. He'd be like all Max's family — Harvard educated and smart as a whip. That would be worse than talking to Detective Scott. And despite lawyer/client privilege, I'd wonder what the lawyer was telling the family.

"Okay." I didn't meet Max's eyes, just studied his very firm chin. He had a nice chin, with a tiny, little cleft right in the middle.

"Is there anything else you need to tell me?" he asked.

My gaze snapped up to his. "Like did I murder him? Is that what you mean?"

He closed his eyes for a second, rubbing the bridge of his nose. Then he crossed the room in three steps and pulled me into his arms. "No, honey. I know you didn't kill him. I just love you so much. The thought of something happening to you makes me crazy. I'm sorry."

Well, I'd succeeded in distracting him, but now I felt worse. With his words, he heaped red coals of shame upon my head. How much more could I take? I had to find my answers and fast.

9

With my arms full of yearbooks, a bag from the drugstore, and my purse, I brushed past a surprised Abbie at her front door. I was out of breath from running up the stairs. She lived above an antique shop in the middle of town.

I dumped everything on her taupe leather sofa, whirled around, and faced her. "I have another interview with Detective Scott today." I glanced at my watch. "In exactly ninety minutes. I need you to help me prepare. I hope you have some time. If you'd answer your phone or get a cell phone, I'd be able to get in touch with you."

She shut her front door and faced me. "I was in the shower, so I didn't hear the answering machine. And I hate cell phones."

"I brought bribes." I pointed at the stuff I'd dropped. "I also brought a notebook to make notes in. And I have all of Russ's yearbooks. I need to make a list of things to distract the police so I have more time to check into Russ's past and see who was blabbing to Jim Bob."

"Have you talked to Max yet?" she asked.

"No." I met her gaze. "I tried. Then Karen walked in and started talking about her mother. I couldn't do it after that."

She studied my face a moment more; then she glided to the couch and fished through the plastic bag, pulling out two plain stenographer's pads and six Cadbury eggs. She grinned and bounced an egg on her palm. "My very favorite. You're serious about bribery, I see. Are they all for me?"

I nodded.

She waved a pad in the air. "Couldn't you have gotten notebooks that were a little more decorative?"

I took it from her. "This is serious business. I didn't want to show up at Detective Scott's office with something that had pink and purple fairies on the cover."

She continued to bounce the egg in her hand. "Okay. Here's the deal. I'll help you if you promise to talk to Max within the next week."

"I want to. I'm trying." I crossed my arms. "Why are you so insistent about this?"

"I don't want anything to happen to you guys. Remember my short marriage? My ex was keeping secrets."

"Yeah, but his secret was two women on the side. He betrayed you."

"Don't you think Max will feel betrayed by something like this?"

I raked my fingers through my hair. "Yes. Yes, he will. I know that. That's what makes this hard. But if Russ is guilty, then my step-kids are going to hate me. And . . . I don't know how Max will feel. I mean . . ." My throat closed up, and tears filled my eyes.

"Oh, hon, I'm sorry." Abbie hugged me. "I don't think you're giving everyone enough credit, but I don't know for sure."

I sniffled into her shoulder for a minute until I got hold of myself.

"Let's get to work." She motioned to the dining room table. "But I have my doubts that you'll be able to distract Eric."

Once again, I sensed the edge in her voice when she mentioned his name. Abbie's ex-husband had been a police officer. As we sat down, a thought occurred to me. I glanced at her. "Is the reason you don't like Detective Scott because he reminds you of your ex-husband?"

Abbie raised her chin, and her eyes looked like flint. "Eric went to the academy with him. They were friends. He has a lot of nerve judging me when he and his wife split up, too." She huffed. "I don't want to discuss it, okay?"

"Okay." I knew better than to ask anything else. She'd tell me in her own good time.

I opened a notebook and pulled a pen from my purse. "I think Jim Bob was a blackmailer. He was trying to blackmail me. And he tried to pull something on George."

"Well, most everyone agrees he wasn't a nice guy." The corner of Abbie's mouth twitched. "Which could explain why Stefanie did what she did."

I eyed Abbie. "What did she do?"

"Well, at the hairdresser yesterday, I heard whispers about her and Daryl."

I remembered Shirl's comment about sneaky men. "You're not saying that Daryl and Stefanie . . ."

Abbie raised an eyebrow. "The Bible calls it adultery."

"That's hard to believe." I shuddered. "I mean, we're talking about Daryl."

She shrugged. "If you didn't know him like you do, you'd think he was quite good-looking."

The Dweeb? Good-looking? I couldn't get past the gross little boy I'd known in grade school.

"Right there are some mighty good motivations." Abbie crossed her legs. "You've got lust and anger and greed."

"I get the lust and anger part, but greed?"

"Sure. Maybe Stefanie thought Daryl could get a piece of his wife's fortune."

If I'd been a cartoon character, there would be a lightbulb over my head. "Of course. She was looking for her next well-to-do guy. Or at least one with the potential." There weren't many in our area, really. Daryl, Max, although his family didn't have as much as Daryl's wife's . . . oh . . . Max.

I clenched my fists. "She's been flirting with Max, trying to get into Jim Bob's storage unit. Do you suppose she wants more than that?"

"From what I've heard, I'd say that if Max succumbed she'd jump in with both feet."

I couldn't speak.

Abbie looked at me with a tiny grin. "Trish, close your mouth. You'll catch flies."

I snapped my jaw shut and said nothing. Though some of my suspicions about Steffie were vindicated, Abbie's words triggered my latent insecurity. I, Trish Cunningham, redneck and the daughter of a struggling farmer, had married Maxwell Cunningham the Third, third child and only son of a wealthy family. No one could have predicted such a match. He was way out of my league. Something his mother had hinted at on more than one occasion, making it difficult for me to forget. Now, if my brother had been responsible for Max's first wife's death . . . well, I would never live that down.

I forced my mind from the Cunninghams and back to the problem at hand. "Okay, so Daryl and the not-so-grieving widow could have been in cahoots. I know she wasn't at the store that morning — at least not as far as I know — but Daryl was. And Gail says that Daryl was at the doctor's that afternoon. He needed stitches."

Abbie nodded. "Make a note of that. And what about Frank?"

"You heard about the embezzling?" I asked.

"Yes, but he hasn't been charged yet."

"He's still a tattletale like he was in school. He told Detective Scott about me and Jim Bob. I also wonder if he's the one who said something to Jim Bob about Russ."

She scooted next to me. "Let's check out Russ's friends."

We opened the yearbook for his senior year. The front flap had a dedication to Daryl's little brother Tim, who had drowned in a lake.

"That was so sad," I said. "Russ and Tim were good friends, you know. Tim was a bad influence. He always got away with stuff because his folks and Daryl doted on him."

She glanced at me. "Then put his name on your list."

I did. Then feeling a little like a voyeur, I glanced at all the inscriptions that Russ's friends had written. I tapped a finger on one. "I had forgotten this. Russ dated Peggy Nichols."

"Really?"

"Yep. He broke her heart."

"We'll ask her some questions on Saturday, then." Abbie flipped through more pages. "I had forgotten that Lee Ann's husband, Norm, had hung out with Russ."

"Me, too."

Abbie glanced at her watch. "You need to go. Cops don't like to be kept waiting." She grinned ever so slightly. "However, they do like to keep you waiting. Be prepared to sit in the lobby. It's a tactic to keep you off guard."

Abbie's warning served me well. I arrived fifteen minutes early. Fifteen minutes after my scheduled appointment, Corporal Fletcher walked through the door into the lobby.

"Sorry to keep you waiting, Mrs. C."

I narrowed my eyes. How many people called me Mrs. C.? Shirley? The people who worked for me and Max?

"Come on in." He held open the door to the inner sanctum of the sheriff's office as though inviting me into his home. "You want something to drink? A Coke? Some water?"

"No, thank you, Corporal Fletcher," I said through stiff lips.

He had the nerve to smile at me as he directed me toward some stairs and motioned for me to go up ahead of him. "Detective Scott is waiting for you."

"Is he now?" My irritation level rivaled my nervousness.

The corporal said nothing else, just directed me to the same interview room where I'd been questioned before. Detective Scott was already there and stood as I entered. I noticed several files on the table, as well as a notepad and a pen.

"Hello, Mrs. Cunningham. Please have a seat. Did Corporal Fletcher offer you something to drink?"

"Yes. I don't want anything, thank you."

He nodded at the corporal, who shut the door, leaving me alone with the detective. He motioned for me to sit in a chair. As he sat opposite me, I pulled my notebook from my bag. "I have some thoughts for you." I flipped to the first page and ran my finger down my list. "I've been investigating."

"What?" he demanded.

I glanced up at him, meeting his frowning gaze. "I said I've been investigating. I've gathered some information for you."

His silence told me a lot. I'd startled him. That was good. I wanted to keep him off balance for a change.

"Well, I've jotted down some things that I've heard. Like, did you know that Jim Bob Jenkins was a blackmailer? He tried to blackmail George." I put the steno pad on the table and tapped it with my index finger. "And Daryl Boyd was supposedly sleeping with Stefanie. She was out for money, you know. At least that's the theory."

Detective Scott leaned toward me. "Mrs. Cunningham, you can't investigate this —"

I waved a hand in the air. "Call me Trish, please. And I'm only collecting information to give to you. You're the detective."

His lips narrowed. "This is a murder investigation."

"Yes. I know. I'm the one who found Jim Bob, which makes me a suspect, too. I don't want to be a suspect, so I'm collecting information."

"No one is accusing you of anything," he pronounced. Again.

I snorted. "This is the third time I've been

here, Detective. Max is worried. He wants to get me a lawyer." I picked up my pad of paper and brandished it like a fan. "As I see it, there aren't too many people who could be the killers." I frowned. "Except if a perfect stranger came in through the side door. Do you think that Jim Bob and Daryl left the side door open?"

I glanced at Detective Scott out of the corner of my eyes.

He leaned back in his chair and tapped his pen on the table slowly. It sounded like a second hand on a clock. "Trish, when did you last speak to Jim Bob Jenkins?"

I dropped the notebook on the table. "Well, I talked to him at the Shopper's Super Saver. And you know what? As far as I can tell, there are three main suspects. Besides me, of course —"

"Was that the last time you spoke to him?" Detective Scott's voice was low and insistent. *Tap, tap, tap, tap.*

The sound of his pen was worse than water torture. A suspect would talk just to get him to stop doing that.

I flipped the paper in my notebook. "Well, I told you that I saw him in the parking lot at the grocery store and —"

Tap, tap, tap, tap.

"Trish, where did you last speak to Jim

Bob Jenkins?"

Abbie was right. Detective Scott was not distractible. I finally met his gaze. He knew. The fact that Corporal Fletcher called me Mrs. C. was my first clue. He'd probably done it on purpose to let me know they'd been to Four Oaks Self-Storage to investigate. We had cameras that recorded the office and grounds twenty-four hours a day. Not sound, just pictures. The police could have easily viewed those. If I lied, things would be much worse for me than they already were.

I bowed my head and felt tears prickling in my eyes. "Last Friday," I whispered.

I heard his breath escape in a tiny sigh as though he'd been holding it, waiting for me to tell him the truth. He put the pen down. "Can you tell me about that?"

His voice was gentle, and that was worse than anything else. Tears spilled over my lower eyelids. I swiped hard at them. I hate crying. I'd rather fight.

"Do I have to?" I sniveled and fought for control.

"It would be best if you did," he said.

"Confession is good for the soul" is a platitude that my mother used when I was young to make me tell her all the things I'd done wrong. It lost its meaning early in my life because I realized that she would use my confessions against me at some point in the future. However, in the case of me and Detective Scott, the saying held true to a degree. After spilling my guts to him, I felt a small sense of relief. Maybe that was simply because I no longer feared that deputies would show up at my door to arrest me. At least not right now. I was sure I was still on the suspect list, but telling the truth goes a long way.

So, it was with a semilighter heart that I rushed into the school auditorium on Saturday morning, trailed by Max and Tommy, who carried my stuff in boxes. That I would be in charge of a healthy-heart booth at a health fair was a little ironic, considering my mother made a living selling heart attacks. That's probably why I allowed myself to be coerced into doing it. To be fair, people needed to be warned of the dangers of consuming too much fat. Then, fairly warned, they could eat doughnuts, and I wouldn't have to feel vicariously guilty.

Max and Tommy left everything at my table and took off. Abbie was already there, dressed in an ivory pantsuit, talking with the principal of the school, Peggy Nichols, my brother's onetime girlfriend. They both turned when we arrived and greeted us. Then a bald custodian walked by. He looked like the man I'd seen at the baseball game.

"Who is that?" I asked, pointing in his direction.

"Peter Ramsey, the custodian," Peggy said. "Will you excuse me, please? I need to speak with him."

Maybe that explained his attendance at the game. Sometimes school custodians hired out to help at other functions.

"Hi, Abs," I said as I placed a box on a battered particleboard table.

"Hi, hon."

I covered the table with a pretty cloth; then Abbie and I quickly set up everything else. I glanced around the room. During the week, it served as a cafeteria. Beige-painted, cinder-block walls were the backdrop for the event. More tables filled the room this year, but I couldn't figure out which were the new ones. Although the event was called a health fair, it had evolved into much more than that. Now, in addition to the local dentist, doctor, and hospital, the sheriff's department had a table, as well as other community organizations.

As people began to arrive, Abbie sat on one stool, while I perched on the other. We surreptitiously ate doughnuts, which she'd picked up from Ma's.

"Detective Scott knows about Jim Bob, me, and Russ," I said through a mouthful of glazed doughnut. "He knew before I told him."

Abbie nodded. "That doesn't surprise me."

"He promised he would look into Lindsey's death for me. Maybe it was solved or something and Jim Bob was just using it to try to get free storage. Then he told me I have to talk to Max."

"Good. So when are you going to talk to Max?"

I bit my lip and sighed. "Well, today is shot. He's going shopping with Sammie and Charlie tonight. Sammie's getting a new hamster. I want the timing to be perfect. No chance for interruptions. Tomorrow we're eating dinner at my folks, so I'm thinking that I'll leave the little kids there, and Max and I can go out tomorrow night."

"That sounds like a good plan," she said. Then she frowned. "Frank is here. With his kids."

I followed her gaze. He was at one of the other tables. "His kids go to school here. I guess he decided not to hide out in shame. Maybe he's not guilty."

"Well, his wife kicked him out, and he's

living with his parents. He's no longer employed at Shopper's Super Saver. He probably doesn't have anything else to do."

I felt a tug of sympathy for Frank. "How do you know all this stuff, Abs? You're like a walking encyclopedia of Four Oaks."

She winked. "I make it my business to know things. And I suspect Jim Bob was also hassling Peggy Nichols."

"Why?"

"Because earlier I expressed my concern that we had a murderer loose in Four Oaks. She snarled and said lots of people had reason to see Jim Bob dead, and then she clammed up."

Abbie's gaze lifted over my head, and her face grew tight. I turned and saw Detective Scott approaching the table.

"Why are you here?" I asked rudely. I'd never seen him in a uniform. Usually he wore a suit, and I found the change a bit intimidating.

"I'm taking my turn at the Sheriff's Department table." He didn't seem to take offense at my tone. "We're fingerprinting little kids." His eyes flickered over Abbie.

"Eric," she said coolly.

He nodded slightly then looked at me. "Trish, may I have a word with you for just a moment?"

I felt my stomach lurch.

"Go ahead," Abbie said. "I'll man the table."

"Thanks a lot," I mouthed to her.

Detective Scott walked me out of the auditorium and into the hallway. I imagined how this would play out later with Rumors 'R Us. We stopped in front of the school office. An appropriate location, since it's where the principal's office was, and the way he took me out of the auditorium reminded me of all the times I'd been yanked out of class when I was young and in trouble.

I looked up at him. "Are you going to arrest me now?"

He shook his head. "If I were going to arrest you, I wouldn't politely walk you from the room." He paused. "I looked into Lindsey's death. The case is still open."

I felt like throwing up. "What does that mean?"

He took a deep breath. "Whoever took that sign is probably guilty of involuntary manslaughter. There's no statute of limitations on that, I'm afraid."

I swallowed. "So Russ could be arrested?"

Detective Scott shrugged. "If he's guilty. But we don't know that. Yet. I'm looking into anything that has to do with Jim Bob Jenkins and his murder." The detective paused and gazed down at me. I thought I saw some concern there. "Trish, you need to tell Max about your brother. And just as important, stay away from the murder investigation. Someone is playing for keeps."

"Does that mean I'm not a suspect?"

His expression turned blank. "I told you, you're not accused of anything. You'll know if I change my mind."

Tommy came to help clean up; then he would take me home. He, Abbie, and I carted stuff back and forth until everything was packed in the car. A group of deputies walked by, along with Detective Scott. He saluted me.

"You ready to go, Mom?" Tommy asked.

"Just about. I need to run to the bathroom real fast." I glanced at Abbie. "Thanks for helping, Abs."

"I had a good time, as usual," she said.

After she hugged me, she walked to her red Mustang, passing right by Detective Scott. She acknowledged him with a slight dip of her head and kept walking with a stiff back. He watched until she climbed into her car.

"Mom?" My son's voice pulled me from my observations. "You going to the ladies room?"

I turned and smiled at him. "Yeah. I'll be right back."

The halls were empty when I ran into the bathroom. I used the facilities and freshened my lipstick. Then I charged back out into the hallway.

"Looking for more bodies?"

I skidded to a stop and turned around. Frank stood there, hands in his pockets and a scowl on his face.

I crossed my arms and glared at him. "That's a horrible thing to say. Why are you here?"

"To talk to you." He stared down at me, jingling change in his pocket. "Did you tell the cops about the knife?"

"What? You mean the one in Jim Bob? Of course." I stared at him. Why was he asking this?

"Did it look like a meat cutter's knife?" he asked.

"Come on, Frank. I have no idea what a meat cutter's knife looks like. Now, I'm tired of talking." I turned to leave.

"You talk enough to the cops." He said the words softly, but I sensed terrible anger in the tone.

I whirled around to face him again. "Can I help it if they keep asking me questions?"

Briefly, I felt like we were kids in grade

school again, fighting on the playground. The lights flickered and went off. I heard voices in the distance; then they stopped. The only illumination came from windows in the classrooms. The twilightlike atmosphere heightened my senses. I smelled chalk and floor wax. The dim hallway loomed in both directions like an endless tunnel going nowhere. Frank's rapid breathing and the beating of my heart matched paces. I no longer felt like a kid.

I heard the sound of footsteps behind me. Frank stood at attention and backed up. I turned around. My stepson was trotting down the hall.

"Mom? Is everything okay?" he asked.

My breath whooshed out in relief. "Yes. Everything is fine." Now.

Frank said nothing, just walked past us and hurried away. I linked my arm in Tommy's as we walked down the hall. Frank had made me feel cold. I needed the comfort of human touch.

Tommy glanced down at me. "I was worried because Dad said you haven't been feeling well."

"Thank you. I'm glad you came."

We reached the foyer, and I welcomed the sunlight. "That was Frank, right?" Tommy asked.

I nodded.

He opened the door and waited for me to pass by. “He was putting off some seriously bad vibes, Mom.”

That had occurred to me, too. “I think he blames me for his problems. He’s just looking for a scapegoat.”

Tommy glanced at me. “If he thinks that, he’s an idiot.”

I’d always thought so, despite trying hard not to. I’d just never seen his creepy side.

10

Sunday mornings had always been one of my favorite times of the week, especially since they reminded me of my courtship with Max. But not this morning. My relief after confessing to Detective Scott had faded, and now I was in the throes of abject misery, feeling sick with worry about talking to Max tonight.

To make matters worse, I taught the five- and six-year-olds the lesson about the dangers of lying. Then the pastor added to my wretched state by continuing a series about family that was leading up to Easter Sunday. Today's was about marriage.

Max grabbed my hand, and the two of us followed Charlie and Sammie to my SUV. Our two oldest had taken off right after church.

"Karen and Tommy will meet us at your folks', right?" Max asked.

"Yep. Tommy has a big exam tomorrow,

so he's not staying long after lunch. And Karen is going to see Julie."

After the kids were settled in the vehicle, Max opened my door. As I climbed in, my steno pad slipped out from under the seat where I'd put it.

Max grabbed it. After a quick glance, he frowned and held it up. "What is this?"

"Nothing much." I tried to snatch it from his hand, my heart pounding.

He held it out of my reach and flipped it open. "This looks suspiciously like —"

"Nothing," I said. "It's not important. It's old. I was just sort of downloading thoughts last week." I held my hand out.

He narrowed his eyes and didn't give me the notebook. "You're not still involved in all this, are you? You told me Eric Scott said you weren't a suspect."

I lowered my hand and shrugged. "What do you mean by *involved?*"

I got a glittery-eyed glance. "You're avoiding the question. A simple yes or no would do. Frankly, I want you to leave the whole thing behind."

How could I leave it all behind? "You're being overprotective and maybe even a little bossy."

"What?" He ran his other hand through his hair. "I'm not . . ." He glanced at the children.

I turned to look at them, too. Two pairs of bright eyes stared at us. I'm always amazed at how children listen when they aren't supposed to and ignore the things they're supposed to listen to.

Max said nothing else, just handed me the notebook and helped me into the SUV, shut my door, and climbed into the driver's side. We didn't speak as he drove from the parking lot. I had a feeling the topic would come up again.

When we'd gotten premarital counseling, the pastor had given us tests, so he could determine our strengths and weaknesses. Max rated pretty high in bossiness, although they called it something else that didn't sound quite so negative. He tried his best to watch his attitude with me, but he wasn't always successful.

A couple of minutes later, he reached over and squeezed my hand. "Remember we talked about that convention in Chicago?"

I nodded.

"I've decided I have to go. I need to see the programs and try them before we buy. It starts on Monday afternoon."

I bit my lip. That didn't give me much time to get ready, but a trip would give me more time alone with Max than just this evening. It was perfect. "Okay, I can be packed by tonight. I'm sure Mom and Dad will watch the kids."

He glanced at me, surprise on his face. "What are you talking about?"

"I'm thinking out loud." I smiled at him, but he wasn't smiling back.

His attention went to the road while he turned a corner; then he turned back to me. "Why would you think that you're going with me?"

Panic gripped my chest. "You're joking, right?"

"No, I'm not." His hands tightened on the steering wheel. "I thought we agreed yesterday that you couldn't leave right now."

Yesterday? Had I said that? Had we agreed? I couldn't remember. And I couldn't believe he was going without me. When was I going to talk to him?

"I know this isn't a good time to leave you, but with the expansion, I need to shop programs and other things now." His words came out in a rush.

"Max, I thought we were both going."

He ran a hand through his hair. "I've already booked my flight. I'm sorry. I thought we agreed."

I wanted to stomp my feet on the floor.

"We didn't agree at all. Why are you leaving me?"

The vehicle had become deathly quiet. Max glanced in the rearview mirror. I could feel the children leaning forward in their seats, waiting to see who said what next.

"Let's discuss it later," I said quietly, although I was screaming on the inside.

He nodded. "Good idea."

My agenda for the evening was shot. As my mother would say, "The best-laid plans of mice and men . . ."

When we walked into her kitchen, the steamy air was fragrant with the smell of potatoes and roast. My father was leaning against the counter. I met his wide smile with one of my own. Besides Max, my father is the most important man in my life. He crossed the room in three steps to hug me. I clung to him for a beat longer than I usually did. He looked down at me with narrowed eyes but said nothing. He had always been able to read me — sometimes too well. If we'd been alone, he would have probed to find out what was wrong.

The huge dining room table was loaded with food. Ma served roast beef with all the trimmings. The only sounds I heard for the first few minutes were forks clinking against plates as we all ate. Everyone except Karen, who had been moping all morning. That didn't go unnoticed by my mother.

"What's ailin' you, Karen?" she finally asked.

Karen twirled her fork in her mashed potatoes and sighed dramatically. "Nothing."

"Hah!" Charlie said. "She's upset 'cause her best friend wants to run away."

That sounded serious. I wondered if Lee Ann knew.

"You shut up," Karen said to Charlie. "At least I'm not a freak who sees ghosts."

"Karen . . . ," Max warned.

"What are you talking about?" Charlie yelled.

"All your talk about dead people," she said.

"What do you know anyway, so busy talking on the phone and —"

"That's enough," Max said sternly. His order, combined with his frown, made an impression. The kids quieted — for a moment.

My mother and father, along with Sammie, watched Charlie and Karen with wide eyes.

Tommy, who was so busy stuffing his face that I didn't think he'd noticed anything, waved his fork in the air. "Sometimes I think

Charlie knows more than we all give him credit for."

"What?" Karen yelped. "You're crazy. So is he. My whole family is crazy. A total embarrassment. I should just leave with Julie."

"I said, that's enough." Max's angry tone and glittering eyes left no question in anyone's mind that he meant what he said.

"More gravy, Tommy? Mashed potatoes?" My mother asked brightly, as if gravy and potatoes would fix everything.

"Daddy's going, too, like Julie," Sammie piped up. "He's leaving Mommy."

The silence that followed her statement was louder than Karen yelling. I can safely say that children hear everything, but important facts get lost in the translation.

"What she means is, Max is going out of town," I said, trying to keep my voice neutral.

My mother dropped her fork to her plate. "Out of town? Without you?"

"Yes, without me." I couldn't help the way my voice wavered.

"Well, I never. I thought the two of you were attached at the hip." She glanced from me to Max. "If you ask me, it'll be good for you. Too much togetherness is unhealthy."

I hadn't asked her. And it wasn't like Max

and I had time to really be together. I'd married a man with three children. We'd hardly had a honeymoon to speak of because Charlie had been so little at the time and we didn't want to leave him for long. Automatic family. Now, with four kids and a growing business, not to mention our church activities, running the kids around, and things like ball games, we had very little time alone together. I opened my mouth to express my thoughts, but Daddy must have seen the anger in my eyes.

He cleared his throat. "So, Max, where are you going?"

"Chicago. To a self-storage convention." Max went on to explain in great detail why he was going and what he needed to accomplish.

He probably wanted me to listen so I'd understand, but I didn't. Instead, I twirled my mashed potatoes like Karen. Now when would I get a chance to talk to him? Tonight he'd want to spend time with the family. Plus, he was leaving me stuck at home alone with quarreling children. I felt his gaze on me but didn't look up. I was not a happy camper.

Monday night, after the kids were in bed, I pulled on one of Max's sweatshirts instead of pajamas and retrieved my steno pad. While I waited for him to call me, I'd organize all my clues. Maybe while he was gone, I could come up with some answers. I'd been right about having no time to talk to him the night before. Besides, telling him that my brother had possibly killed his first wife wasn't something I wanted to drop on him before a business trip.

I reviewed the notes I'd taken at Abbie's, starting with Russ's friends. I didn't remember much about my brother's life back then. I was ten years older. Tim, Peggy Nichols, Norm. I bit the end of my pen. Was it possible that Tim had stolen the stop sign and Daryl told Jim Bob that Russ did it just to protect his dead brother? And maybe Peggy still had sour grapes over Russ dumping her. She'd never married. Was it possible to carry a torch that long? Then there was Norm. He was a bit older than Russ, but they used to hang out together during the summer. That's all I knew, which frustrated me, so I flipped a page. I'd work on Jim Bob's murder instead.

As soon as I'd written MOTIVATIONS in big letters, the phone rang. I snatched it from the bedside table, dropping my steno pad on the floor in my hurry.

"Hello? Max?"

"Hi, baby." His voice on the phone is even better than in person. Low and intimate. Just hearing it through the receiver makes my insides feel like warm syrup. "I miss you. I hate sleeping alone."

"Me, too. So . . . are you . . . having a good time?" I hoped not.

"*Good time* isn't the right word. I'm getting things done. I think I've found a new computer program, but I wanted to talk it over with you before I buy it."

"Tell me," I said, settling back against the headboard.

He talked for about thirty minutes. We discussed the pros and cons.

"What do you think?" he asked.

I agreed with his choice.

Silence fell between us. I was afraid to speak because I might cry.

"Trish, what's wrong?" Max asked. "Has Eric been in touch with you again?"

"No, but . . . Max, we need to talk." I picked at the sheet.

He paused. "I thought we were talking."

"No, I have something we need to talk about. In person. That's why I wanted to go to Chicago with you."

I heard him breathing; then he inhaled. "Are you okay? Did you go to the doctor?"

I almost laughed, realizing where his mind

was going. He thought I was ill. "I'm fine. It's nothing like that."

He took a deep breath. "I want you to go to the doctor, okay?"

I didn't answer, because I didn't intend to go. But I did feel bad for Max. He's so self-assured that I sometimes forget he's got vulnerabilities.

"I'm serious, Trish."

"Okay, okay," I grumbled.

He sighed. "Are you sure you don't want to discuss whatever it is right now?"

"Yes. I'm sure."

He sighed again. "All right. Get some sleep. I'll call you tomorrow."

I slept fitfully, thrashing around in bed. At around two in the morning, I woke with my covers and legs twisted together like a pretzel. I untangled myself and rolled over on my back. Something banged against the side of the house. I sat up. Then I heard another sound, like scratching. Was the wind blowing? My heart pounded. I held my breath and listened.

Nothing. I waited. Still nothing.

But now I was wide awake and would most likely toss and turn with guilt if I tried to sleep. Maybe I should eat a peanut butter and jelly sandwich. Nothing says comfort like peanut butter and jelly.

I pulled on a pair of jeans to wear with Max's sweatshirt, slid into my favorite old bunny slippers, and crept down the stairs. All the kids were asleep. Everything was dark except for a tiny night-light next to the front door. I walked down the hallway, scuffing my slippers on the wood floor. Then I heard scratching again.

It's the wind, I told myself. But it continued, sounding like dog nails on the front door. Our front door is massive. One of those solid metal doors with tiny little windows at the top. It also has a really nice doorknob. Brass. And it was jiggling.

11

"I'm calling the police right now, so you'd better back off," I yelled as I jerked on the lights to the hall and the porch. Praying under my breath, I backed down the hallway, hands on the wall, feeling my way to the kitchen. After almost falling over the doorjamb, I turned and fumbled for the light switch and turned it on. Then I snatched the cordless phone from its bed on the wall and dialed 9-1-1.

Even while dispatch answered, I crept back up the hallway. I had to protect my children from whoever was trying to break in. But the doorknob had stopped moving.

After I explained what was going on, the dispatcher cautioned me not to open the door. Like I'm that stupid.

I assured her I was staying put; then I got a beep telling me I had another call. I ignored it and sat on the bottom step, watching the doorknob. Still no movement.

She kept me on the phone until squad cars with flashing lights filled my driveway and deputies were at the door.

I flung it open. Detective Eric Scott stood there, face scruffy with beard growth, dressed in jeans and a dark blue sweatshirt. He would have looked almost human except for the gun on his waist and his eyes, which were squinting at me.

"I didn't do anything," I said automatically.

"What?" He rubbed his face then shook his head. "I know that. We need to come in and check things out. Are you okay?"

Mad, scared, heart still pounding, but . . . "Yes." I stood back.

The detective came in, followed by Corporal Fletcher and a younger deputy.

"We'll check things out, Sarge," the corporal said.

"Good." Detective Scott nodded.

"My kids are asleep," I said.

"Not all of them." Corporal Fletcher motioned behind me.

I turned; Tommy, clad only in jeans, was tromping down the stairs, followed by Karen in a bathrobe.

"What's going on, Mom?" Tommy asked.

"Someone tried to break in," I said. "Are Charlie and Sammie still in bed?"

Karen nodded.

Detective Scott glanced at the corporal. "Fletcher, I want you outside to supervise, okay?"

"Yes, sir." Corporal Fletcher turned and walked off the porch.

"Is there somewhere we can sit?" the detective asked.

I nodded and led the way to the kitchen where I slumped into a chair, placing the phone on the table. I felt Tommy's presence at my back. Karen was leaning against the counter, twirling her hair in her fingers.

I rubbed my eyes and explained everything.

When I was done, Detective Scott took a deep breath. "Are you aware that someone tried to break into the offices of Four Oaks Self-Storage tonight?"

"What?" Tommy barked behind me. "Mom, we gotta call Dad."

"In a minute, Tommy." I didn't want to talk to Max until I'd totally calmed down. I wondered if the beep I'd ignored had been the alarm company trying to call me about the attempt at the storage offices.

"Did they get in?" Tommy asked, sounding very much like his father.

"No," the detective said.

About that time, I heard Charlie's voice.

"Mom! Where are you?" He stormed into the kitchen, face squished up with fear. "What is going on around here? There are cops upstairs and cop cars outside."

"Someone tried to break in the house, but it's okay." I attempted to sound reassuring, feeling anything but. Things weren't okay. My fear was dissipating, leaving behind only anger. I needed to talk to the detective. I turned to the children. "Would you three mind giving me a few minutes alone with Detective Scott? Karen, go check on Sammie. Charlie, if she wakes up, don't you dare scare her with this. I mean it."

Karen nodded and left the room.

Charlie bounced next to me. "Mom, can I —"

"Charlie," I snapped. "Just go away, okay?"

He ran from the room. I had a feeling he was going outside to watch the activity. I didn't try to stop him.

Tommy didn't move. I turned and looked up at him.

His jaw was set. "Mom, I'd really like to stay. Dad sort of left me in charge."

I didn't want any of the kids in here in case Detective Scott said something about Russ. "I appreciate your concern for me, but I think perhaps the other kids could use your strength right now."

"I think I should stay," he said, crossing his arms.

I met his gaze and shook my head. We had a silent battle of wills, a stare down of sorts. He finally looked away. Then he put his shoulders back and gave the detective a steely glance. "All right. But if you need me for anything, call."

Detective Scott watched him leave. "Tommy really watches out for you."

"Just what I need — another keeper," I grumbled as I waved at a chair. "Why don't you sit down?"

He did.

"Would you like coffee, Detective?"

"Yes, please," he said. "Black."

I busied myself fixing it, my anger growing by the second. When the liquid started to drip into the carafe, I whirled around. I guess the anger showed on my face or in my gaze because his eyes widened.

With as much dignity as I could muster, given that I was wearing fuzzy pink bunny slippers with crossed eyes and Max's sweatshirt, which hung to my knees, I decided to tell the detective what I thought. "It was Stefanie Jenkins."

"What?" He fastened his sharp gaze on my face. "Did you see her?"

"Well, no."

"Why do you think that?"

I crossed my arms. "Because she wants to get into Jim Bob's storage unit and will use any method possible, including offering to do anything for Max. We're both adults, and I'm sure you understand like I do what that means. She tries to act nice, but I don't believe her. Do you think a little locked door is going to keep her from trying to steal a key? Not to mention, she was probably hoping Max would be here alone or something."

The detective's mouth twitched as though he wanted to laugh. I wasn't amused. I filled a mug with black coffee and clunked it down in front of him. Then I got some for me and sat at the table.

"So how could she have been in two places at once?" He lifted his coffee to his lips, watching me over the rim of the cup.

"How should I know? But I'm sure if she could offer favors to Max, she's capable of offering the same thing to someone else to help her." I leaned forward. "What's in that unit that she wants so bad?"

Detective Scott watched me.

"You know, she married him for his money. That's the only thing that makes sense because he wasn't exactly the studly kind of guy that a looker like Stefanie would be attracted to. Everyone says he was ugly. Of course, ugly is as ugly does, as my mother would say. Steffie probably killed him." I paused, took a sip of coffee, and put the cup down. "Then there's Frank. Maybe Jim Bob knew about the embezzling and threatened Frank. He is a creep. I didn't know that before, but now I do. I guess if he could embezzle and be creepy then murder wouldn't be out of the question." I frowned at the detective. "I have trouble imagining the Dweeb guilty of murder."

Detective Scott set his mug down hard. "The Dweeb?"

"Daryl. He's been the Dweeb since kindergarten." I tapped a finger on my mug. "I heard he was having an affair with Stefanie. That surprised me because I know his wife."

"Sarge!" Corporal Nick "Santa Cop" Fletcher burst into the kitchen. "We got signs of attempted entry in a number of places, including windows. Looks like whoever it was tried to use a credit card to open the front door.

I took a huge swig of coffee, nearly half the cup, and suddenly had a brilliant thought. "Hey, I know how it happened."

Both men stared at me.

"Well, Stefanie did one, and Daryl did the other. He's so used to his wife pushing him around that he could be talked into anything."

Silence filled the room as both men stared at me.

Detective Scott nodded slowly and took another sip of coffee. Then he put his cup down. "You think you'll be okay now?"

I realized he'd been tolerating my blabbering until he was sure I was okay. He wasn't taking me seriously at all. "No, I'm not okay, Detective Scott. All these people have a motive for the murder, just like me. Even my mother. She delivered a free box of doughnuts to Jim Bob every week. The world as I knew it no longer exists. Shopper's Super Saver is not safe. I can't drink milk. I'm sick to my stomach. I don't know the people I thought I did. And Max is in Chicago without me." I blinked back sudden tears.

"You oughta call him, Mrs. C.," Corporal Fletcher said. "I'd want my wife to call me."

"He's in Chicago," I repeated. My stomach gurgled.

"We know." Detective Scott pushed the phone toward me. "Please call him."

I frowned and swiped at my nose with the sweatshirt sleeve. "How did you know where he was?"

"He asked me to make sure you were okay

while he was gone." The detective sighed. "After he threatened to get you a lawyer if I interviewed you again. Have you told him about Russ?"

"No," I murmured as my stomach clenched.

"You need to tell him." Detective Scott rubbed his forehead; then he picked up the phone and held it out to me. "Call him now and tell him you're okay."

"I will, but first . . ." I ran to the bathroom and threw up.

When I'd informed Max of the latest mishap, he'd let loose a spate of words that weren't clear through the receiver. He'd catch an early morning flight home, probably through a friend of his father's or something.

I'm not sure I'd ever heard him quite so upset.

I tried to sleep after everyone left but lay awake, stiff and furious that someone dared try to break into my house. Then I went to work despite total exhaustion but got little done. I couldn't focus on anything except my mystery and Max. After falling asleep at my desk with my chin in my hand and waking up with a palm wet from drool, I went home to wait for him. I'd promised Detective Scott I would tell Max about Russ today. That made me edgy. To distract myself, I retrieved my steno pad and pen and then sat cross-legged on the couch in the family room. I turned to the page I'd started last night.

MOTIVATIONS. Though anyone at the store could have been guilty, I only knew three for sure, although Stefanie could have been behind her husband's murder.

Frank was embezzling. Jim Bob blackmailed people. He could have been blackmailing Frank, and Frank got tired of it.

I made a note. *Frank — embezzling; Jim Bob — blackmailing?*

If the rumors were true about Daryl and he was sleeping with Stefanie, he had motivation. I wrote, *Daryl sleeping with Stefanie? Blackmail? Did she have him do it?* Then I thought about the storage unit. *What does she want so badly?*

What about Lee Ann? I paused and chewed the pen. Maybe she had a boyfriend, and that's what made Norm leave. Jim Bob found out and blackmailed her. I jotted down, *Lee Ann? Boyfriend? Blackmail?*

The roar of a car engine and subsequent screeching brakes distracted me from my list. Max was home. Based on his earlier reaction, I wasn't sure what to expect. The kitchen door opened and slammed.

"Trish?"

"I'm in the family room." I shoved the notebook under a pillow on the couch and stood.

He rushed into the room and grabbed me up in his arms, mumbling a stream of incoherent words. Wrinkles etched his forehead and the skin around his mouth. He looked as scruffy as Detective Scott had the night before.

I buried my head in his chest, smelling the scent of airplanes and hotel in his shirt.

"The kids in school?" he murmured into my hair.

"Yep."

"Are they okay?"

"Yes. Tommy's mad that someone tried something while he was in charge. Sammie didn't even wake up during the whole thing, so she's only heard a modified version of what happened. Charlie spent a couple hours regaling the deputies with his theories about which fugitives from justice on *Mysterious Disappearances* tried to hack their way into our house. And Karen wasn't speaking when she left, so everything's the same with her."

He let go of me and stepped back.

I brushed his scratchy cheek with my

finger. "Would you like some lunch?"

"No. Let's go sit down."

In the family room, he dropped onto the couch and pulled me next to him, but I couldn't enjoy his touch. I knew I had to talk to him about Russ.

"This has been a bad couple of weeks." He tightened his arm around me. "Tell me what happened."

I explained how I'd discovered the moving doorknob and the ensuing events. When I was done, I twisted my hands in my lap. "Have you talked to Detective Scott?"

"Ye–e–s." He drew the vowel out, extending the length of the word. "Why?"

"Did he tell you . . . everything?" My voice faltered.

Max sat very still. "What do you mean by *everything?*"

I didn't look at him. "Like . . . everything?"

He took my chin and lifted, forcing me to meet his gaze. "Do you mean everything as in what you wanted to talk to me about?"

I nodded, swallowed, and blinked back tears.

He brushed hair from my face. "Trish, what is it?"

I gulped and couldn't seem to catch my breath. "Give me a second, okay?"

He shifted so that he could see me. That was when I knew he'd caught sight of my mystery-list notebook. He grabbed it.

"You're still making notes?" he asked, after an interminable silence. "Why?"

"Because I have to figure it all out. That's what I want to talk to you about."

"Solving Jim Bob's murder is Detective Eric Scott's job, not yours." Max enunciated each word. "He's the one with the badge and the gun."

"Yes, but . . . I have to solve this. Jim Bob was trying to blackmail me."

Max's head jerked, and his eyes widened. "What?"

"I'm involved in this up to my eyeteeth. I have to figure things out for me and for our family. I don't want to go to jail. I don't want to lose you." Once I started, the words tumbled out before I could think.

"What are you talking about?" He stared at me like I had the proverbial two heads.

The rapid thumping of my heart and a loud roar in my skull made it hard to talk. Max's face wavered in front of me, but I wasn't sure if it was from tears or if I was about to pass out.

"Trish?"

"Russ might have stolen the stop sign where Lindsey was killed," I whispered.

His mouth hung open for just a moment; then he blinked. "What did you say?"

I cleared my throat and tried to speak louder. "Russ used to steal road signs. You know how the kids are around here. He . . . he might have taken the one where Lindsey was killed. That's what Jim Bob was trying to blackmail me about."

Max stared at me and didn't move. "And you didn't see fit to tell me this before? Trish, what were you thinking?"

His gaze felt like a knife slicing through me. That question was one my mother asked me incessantly when I was young. According to her, I never thought anything through. But before I could speak, the phone rang. I wanted to throw it across the room.

"Let me check and see who that is." He grabbed the receiver from the end table.

"The high school," he said staring at me as he pushed the button to answer. "Hello." His eyes lost their focus. "No, we weren't aware of that." He took a deep breath. "She did what?" He listened awhile longer, lips narrowing and nostrils flaring. "Yes, I understand. Thank you."

When he hung up, his cheeks were drawn. "That was Karen's principal. She skipped school today. Apparently, she called the attendance office this morning pretending to be you and told them she wouldn't be there. Someone saw her and Julie out in the woods near the high school and the library and reported them. I have to go pick her up." He got to his feet and looked down at me. "This really hasn't been a good couple of weeks."

That was an understatement.

12

Breakfast on Wednesday morning was tense. Max and I were treading around each other like two wary dogs. He was angry that I hadn't told him right away about Russ, the stop sign, and Jim Bob's threats. He asked me for time to digest what I'd told him before we discussed it at length again. I had to respect that, but I felt like I was dying inside.

He had also grounded Karen from outside social activities for two weeks, and she let us know how unhappy she was by a variety of methods, including screaming and yelling. She should have been grateful to me. I managed to talk her father into allowing her phone privileges, as well as study time at the library.

She never gave him a reasonable explanation for why she skipped school. It might have been nothing more than teenage rebellion, just like Julie's talk of running way might have been the outward expression of a girl angry that her parents had split up, but I had my doubts.

"Trish, did you remember I have meetings in Baltimore today?" Max asked over his shoulder as he opened the door to the garage to leave.

"Yes," I said, staring at his back.

He turned around. "Can you pick up my suit from the cleaners?"

"Yes."

Even though he had hugged me and kissed me goodbye, I still felt bereft. I didn't realize I was twisting my hands in front of me until he glanced down.

He put his briefcase on the floor, came over to stand in front of me, and put his hands on my shoulders. "Honey, what you told me hasn't changed the fact that I love you. Forever and always. But I have some things to work through, plus there's a whole lot to consider. First, we need to know if it's true."

I stared up at him. He had dark circles under his eyes. He hadn't slept any better than I had.

He pushed a piece of hair from my face. "Listen, I hate to ask you this, given everything that's going on, but could you talk to Julie's mom? See if she has any idea what's going on with the girls?"

I nodded. Right now I'd do anything he asked me, just to make him happy again.

"Thank you," he said. "Maybe it'll help us."

I realized he felt as ineffectual in dealing with Karen as I did, but for different reasons. He was a guy and didn't understand. I had once been a fifteen-year-old girl. I did understand. I was also her stepmother, and that, I suspected, had become a problem for her. Of course, now there was the potential for things to get even worse.

Before I left to take the little kids to school and go to work, I called Lee Ann again and finally reached her. She sounded out of breath. She agreed to meet me that night at Bo's Burger Barn.

"Hi, Mrs. C.," Shirl said when I arrived at work. "You okay?"

"Yeah," I fibbed.

"I made coffee."

"I'm trying to quit." I sifted through yesterday's mail, pulling out bills to pay.

"What?" She stared at me. "You quit drinking coffee? I can't believe that."

"Believe it," I muttered. "My head does." Caffeine withdrawal wasn't pleasant, but after serious consideration, I had come to the conclusion that coffee, in addition to Jim Bob's murder, contributed to my stomach ailment.

"Say, did you know that Peggy Nichols has been dragged down to the sheriff's office almost as many times as you have?" Shirl asked.

I gazed at her in surprise. "Why?"

She shrugged. "No clue. I just heard it from someone who was here this morning." She glanced at her desk where she kept her notepad. "Listen, some guy from the paper called. Said he's coming by to interview you."

I gritted my teeth. "Was his name Carey Snook?"

She nodded.

"I don't want to talk to him." I started for my office. I was in no mood to deal with anybody today, especially a nosy reporter.

"I'm sorry. He hung up before I could get a number to call him back. Caller ID said it was unlisted."

"Not a problem," I hollered from my desk. "I'll take care of it."

I would do so by calling Carey at the newspaper office and telling him to quit bugging me, but when I asked for Carey Snook, I was informed that he didn't work there. He'd never worked there.

Why in the world would someone set up an appointment with me and lie about who he was? I could reach only one conclusion — I was about to have a meeting with a fake.

While I waited for him to arrive, I got a phone call from my mother-in-law. She began by inquiring about my health, sounding solicitous, but in reality she just wanted to let me know she'd heard about my latest escapades and didn't think my behavior was suitable for the wife of someone like Max. For an insane moment, I considered informing her about everything going on. However, the satisfaction of listening to her shriek now wouldn't be worth the price I'd have to pay later.

I paced my office and tried to pray but felt, as my mother would say, the heavens were brass. By the time I saw Mr. Counterfeit Reporter pull into the parking lot, I was in a state.

"Send Mr. Snook into the conference room when he gets inside," I growled as I stomped through the front office.

Standing at the copier, Shirl watched me with raised brows. "Guess I shouldn't offer him anything to drink?"

"No." I must have gestured wildly because she took a step away from me. I didn't apologize, just went on into the conference room to wait.

Shortly after, she brought Carey Snook to the door. "Here he is," she announced and went back to her desk where she plopped in her chair and rolled it to a place where she could see and hear everything.

"Mr. Snook, is it?" I said in greeting.

"Yes, ma'am. Thank you for meeting with me." His smile was oily, like a bad used-car salesman. I really disliked his hair. Today he wore big, black glasses.

His eyes narrowed slightly. "I want to talk about Jim Bob. Like I said the other day, everyone's got secrets. I rather thought you might want to talk to me."

That's when it hit me. Carey Snook somehow knew about me and Jim Bob. I wondered how.

Exhaustion and the conversation with my mother-in-law were to blame for my reaction. I walked over to the door and edged it shut so Shirl couldn't see us. I turned back to him. "Snook. Is that German?"

Carey frowned. I'd caught him off guard.

I smiled. "It's quite unusual. I suppose it's your real name?"

"Of course," he said.

I shook my head. "Those silly people at the paper. I called them. They've never heard of you."

He raised his chin. "I'm a freelancer."

"No, you're not." I put my hands on my hips. "You're lying."

The corners of his mouth turned up. "I'm lying?"

The bell over the front door rang. I studied the man who was studying me, too angry to be afraid. He scratched his head, and I noticed that his hair looked a little off-kilter.

I pointed at it. "Is that a hairpiece?" I moved closer to him. "It is. You don't even have your own hair. That's a good thing for you because it's very ugly." My voice grew louder. "Who are you, anyway?"

Shirl peered around the conference room door. "You okay, Mrs. C.?"

"Yes, but Carey Snook is leaving right now." I was itching to grab at the mop on his head just to see if it came off.

After the briefest pause, he grinned. "You have a good day, Mrs. Cunningham." He lowered his voice so only I could hear him. "I'm sure you'll reconsider talking to me before I talk to your husband's family. I'd rather hear the whole story from you." He brushed past me, knocking me off balance. I grasped the door frame and watched him saunter out the front door.

Shirl's gaze followed him until he disappeared; then she turned to me. "You okay,

Mrs. C.?"

"Yeah, I'm okay." I went out to where she stood and saw Hank, one of our longtime customers, leaning against the counter. When I was in high school, he'd been one of my teachers. I made his life rough for a year. Now he was retired from that and had become a dispatcher for the sheriff's office. Seems like a dispatcher would be the harder job. Then again, dealing with students like me for years might make anything else seem like a piece of cake.

Shirl dropped into her chair. "What was that all about?"

I forced a laugh. "I really couldn't tell you. I'm not sure. He calls himself Carey Snook, and he says he's a reporter. But he doesn't work at the paper, and he wears a hairpiece."

Hank stared at me in amazement. "You haven't tried to attack a fellow like that since you've grown up."

"Oh, for crying out loud," I said impatiently, knowing how this would play out with the rumor mill. "I didn't attack him."

Hank was shaking his head. "You know what they say — 'Still waters run deep.' You can't change Mother Nature." Had Hank been to platitude school with my mother?

"Whatever." I walked past the two of them and into my office where I plopped in a chair and put my head in my hands. Shirl was talking loud enough for me to hear her.

"You know," she said, "it seems like things around here are just going to you-know-where."

I had to agree.

"I'll be just a minute," I told the kids as I pulled up at the dry cleaner's. "I have to get your father's suit."

Sammie and Charlie babbled at each other in the back. Karen was next to me in the passenger seat, but she might as well have been in the next state. She had ignored me when she got in the car, turning her body so she couldn't see me. I snatched up my purse and dug around for my wallet.

"Mom," Charlie said. "I don't like the way she's looking at us."

"Karen, don't stare at the little kids," I said as I put my purse on the floor.

"Oh, good grief," she mumbled.

"Not Karen," Charlie yelped. "Her. On the sidewalk."

I glanced out the windshield and met the gaze of my nemesis over whose arm draped several dry cleaning bags. I wondered if the dry cleaners gave Stefanie Jenkins a discount because there was so little of her clothes to clean.

"Mom, do we know her?" Charlie asked. "I'm sure —"

"Yes, we know her. It's Mrs. Jenkins. I'll be back in a minute."

Charlie was mumbling as I shut the door to the van.

"Trish!" Stefanie greeted me like an old friend. She wore tight, black pants with a tight, cropped, florescent orange knit shirt that showed a great deal of belly. No one should look good in a color like that, but she managed to. Her nails were a darker shade of the same color and matched her lipstick. How did she coordinate everything?

"Hello, Stefanie." I was still shaken up from my run-in with the hairpiece-wearing liar and really didn't feel like dealing with Miss Fancy-Pants.

"Oh, please call me Steffie," she gushed. "I just know we can be good friends."

Not in a million years. "What can I do for you?" I asked.

She gave me a bright smile. "I'm hoping you can convince Maxwell to let me into my storage unit."

I was astounded by her audacity. "I can't do that. It's not yours."

"I just thought you'd have some" — she winked — "powers of persuasion. Your husband is obviously crazy about you."

I was glad that was obvious. "I'm sorry, Steffie. What you're asking is illegal."

I watched anger flash in her eyes; then she forced a smile. "No one has to know; just leave me the key somewhere. It'll be our secret."

I gave her my own forced smile. "I'm sorry. I can't help you."

Her charm had run its course. The gloves were off, and her body vibrated with anger. "I don't believe this. My belongings are in that storage unit, and I'm going to get them out."

I gave her my most withering stare. "You'll do it without my help."

I turned my back to her and went inside to pick up my dry cleaning. After I gave the clerk my ticket, I glanced out the window and saw Stephanie get into a car driven by a man. I squinted at them. Was he the same guy I'd seen at the ball game? The custodian at the school? His profile looked familiar.

"Ma'am?" the clerk said, interrupting my thoughts.

I turned around and paid for Max's suit. By the time I got outside, Stefanie was gone.

13

I met Lee Ann in front of Bo's Burger Barn. She didn't say much, just walked ahead of me. A heavyset greeter seated us, slapping menus on the yellow table and informing us that a server would be with us shortly.

"My treat," I said to Lee Ann as I slid into the chartreuse booth. "Get whatever you want."

She narrowed her eyes. "You don't need to do that. I can buy myself a cup of coffee."

"Sorry," I said. "I wasn't trying to insult you."

She sighed. "I just need to feel like I can do something myself."

Lee Ann had always been moody. Back when we had been in 4-H together, I'd managed to offend her at least once every couple of months. Still, we had some good times together. She'd been a bit like a little sister, something I'd never had.

Our server — Gail's granddaughter, Glenda — bounced up to the booth.

"Hey, Trish." She plunked two glasses of water on the table; then she pulled her ticket book from an apron pocket, along with a pen. "You guys hungry? We got a fried catfish special tonight."

I glanced at Lee Ann who shook her head.

"No, we're not getting much," I said. "Hope that's okay. I just want some onion rings and a Diet Coke." I hoped the soda would give me relief from my headache.

"That's fine." She winked. "Don't matter. You're a celebrity around here anyway. My granny says you're in cahoots with the cops. I've been telling everybody."

Oh, that was just great. "Listen, I'm not in cahoots —"

"Can you give me the scoop about who they suspect? Granny says you're in the sheriff's office, like, every day."

"No," I said. "I —"

"It must be just so thrilling to be in on things like that. I saw a picture of the detective from the sheriff's office on television. He's to die for." She fanned herself with her ticket book and heaved a dramatic sigh. "Good thing you have a hot man at home, huh? Otherwise, it'd be hard to keep your mind on the right things." She rolled her eyes toward the ceiling in an expression of ecstasy. "I just love men in uniforms who carry guns."

Not me. I'd be happier if I never saw another cop uniform in my life. And Detective Scott? To die for? Wouldn't Abbie snort about that?

Glenda finished her flight of rapture and looked at me. "Well, it's good you're close-mouthed. They wouldn't trust you otherwise." She turned to Lee Ann. "Whaddaya want?"

Eyeing Glenda with distaste, Lee Ann ordered coffee.

"Okay. I'll be back."

"So what's all that about?" Lee Ann asked.

I shook my head. "My mother has been telling everyone I'm some sort of police informant. I wish she'd stop because I'm not, although it's true I've been at the sheriff's office a lot. They seem to think I saw something that day, and they're determined to get it out of me." I took a sip of water and met Lee Ann's gaze. "But that's not what I called you to talk about."

Her lips were pursed. "Did Karen say that the girls' skipping school was Julie's fault?"

That explained Lee Ann's attitude. "No, not at all. In fact, she won't talk about it. But Charlie overheard Karen say something about Julie running away. I thought you should know."

Lee Ann's expression relaxed. "I know about that. It's because of her father."

I took a big sip of water. "Well, Karen's got issues, too. Maybe you and I could work together somehow to help them."

Lee Ann nodded. "I think Karen's going through that teenage thing where she's mad because her father remarried. Girls are really emotional like that."

She got it in one.

Glenda brought the drinks. "Yours is on the house," she said to me.

Her remark made me feel bad, especially when Lee Ann glared at Glenda's back as she walked away. After she poured sugar and cream into her coffee, Lee Ann took a deep breath and looked at me. "So what have you heard about me and Norm?"

I shrugged. "Not much, really. Just that Norm left for a while."

"Left? That's not quite what happened." She scowled. "I kicked him out. Did you know he started drinking? He drank at work. During lunch. During his break. Packed straight whiskey in his thermos. Used to sit out there under the trees near the landfill and get drunk. Only problem is, by the time he got home, he was coming down. After all these years, he was turning into my old man."

Ouch. That was bad news. "I'm sorry. I remember how your dad was. Norm always seemed to be the stable one."

"Yeah, he was." Lee Ann said nothing else, just sipped her coffee.

"Well, Karen says you have a boyfriend. That might be a good thing."

Her head jerked up. "A boyfriend? Are you joking?"

"I guess you don't?" I asked.

"Definitely not. I don't ever want to deal with another man again." She stared at me. "You're so lucky."

She'd said that more than once when we were young. In fact, we'd had some competitive moments, with jealousy on both sides. Compared to her home life, mine had been good. At least I wasn't beaten on a regular basis, but still, life hadn't been easy living with someone like my mother.

I decided to change the subject, perhaps dig up some clues for my list. "Hey, has some reporter guy been following you around, asking questions?"

Lee Ann frowned and shook her head.

"He's not a real reporter," I said.

"That's weird. How do you know?"

"I called the paper and asked. He came

by the office, and I confronted him. I think he wears a hairpiece."

She sat back in her seat. "Well, what does he want to know?"

I wondered how much to tell her. "All he'll say is that he's trying to dig up people's secrets. I'd like to know who he really is. The police should probably talk to him."

"Yeah, sounds like it." She took another sip of coffee and then searched through her purse. "Thank you for thinking about Julie. I'll be watching out for her. Everything's going to be okay."

"Do you have to go?" I wanted to ask her more questions.

She nodded and put a couple of bills on the table. "I need to check on her."

I paid our bill and left. Although I'd succeeded in my original goal of warning Lee Ann about Julie's threats, I wasn't able to learn anything to further my quest to solve Jim Bob's murder or to find out if Russ was guilty of Lindsey's death.

I walked out to my SUV, got inside, leaned back, and thought. My thoughts were running over one another in my head. I needed someone to help me sort things out. Abbie. I started my vehicle and headed over to her apartment. I wondered how her book was coming and whether Detective Scott was still helping her with law-enforcement questions. I chuckled as I thought about Glenda's comments. Then bright headlights in my rearview mirror interrupted my woolgathering. After several blocks of this, I wondered if the car was following me. When I pulled over in front of the now closed antique store, I didn't turn my SUV off, in case the other vehicle stopped behind me. It didn't. Instead, it just kept going and made a right turn several streets up from where I was. My imagination was as bad as Charlie's.

The front windows of Abbie's apartment were dark. I should have called first, but she so rarely went out at night that I just expected her to be home. Once again, I wished she had a cell phone. Maybe she was in the back, in her bedroom. I hopped from my vehicle and went to the side of the building where I pulled at a metal door. It scraped open, hinges squealing. I ran up one narrow flight of stairs, turned a corner, and ran up another. Carrying groceries this far had to be a royal pain.

At the top, I went through another metal door to the landing where the entrance to her apartment was. I knocked. No one answered. I dug out my cell phone, which was where it was supposed to be for once. I dialed Abbie's number and heard her phone ringing inside. Then the answering machine kicked on. I leaned against the wall, wanting to growl in frustration. The ceiling lamp above me cast a harsh light on the tan walls. I heard nothing inside her apartment and knocked again. Silence swallowed the sound. I felt a prickle of uneasiness on my neck. A car without a muffler passed by on the street. Then a motorcycle. Then nothing. I suddenly felt very alone and punched my cell phone to dial home.

"Trish?" Max answered. "Are you done talking to Lee Ann?"

Hearing his voice made me feel braver, and I walked down the stairs, through the heavy outside door, and into the night.

"Yeah," I said.

"So are you on your way home?" he asked. "I put the little kids to bed. I want to hear how it went with Lee Ann. And you and I need to talk."

"Okay. Be there in a few." Maybe Max and I could get back on solid ground.

When I got home, he was in his office. Tommy's car was gone. I assumed Karen was hiding in her room, talking on the phone. I peered in at Max.

He looked up, took off his glasses, and put them on the desk. "Hi."

He leaned back. "How did it go?" He sounded hopeful, like my talk with Lee Ann would somehow help us solve the Karen problem.

I shrugged. "She didn't really have anything to say about the situation, only confirming what I suspected. That Karen resents me."

I settled in a brown leather chair, curling my legs underneath me.

He sighed, green eyes dark with worry. "Why, exactly, does she resent you?"

"I'm not her real mother."

We stared at each other. I knew he was thinking what I was thinking. If Russ were to blame in any way for Lindsey's death, then Karen's resentment would deepen. I wasn't sure my relationship with her would ever be the same.

Tension creased his forehead. A black cloud had descended over our house, and I wasn't sure how to counteract it. I was about to suggest we pray and then discuss Russ and the stop sign when I heard Karen's rushed footsteps on the stairs.

The back of my chair faced the door, so when Karen stormed in, she didn't see me. "Dad, you wouldn't believe what Mom did —"

I turned and gazed around the chair. She

stopped, put her hands on her hips, and glared at me.

Max sat still, glancing rapidly from me to Karen and back again. "What were you saying, Karen?" His words were mild, but I wasn't fooled. His jaw tightened in anger.

"Well, she blabbed to Mrs. Snyder that Julie was talking about running away. That wasn't any of her business to tell. Julie got yelled at and everything." Karen scowled through blond bangs. "Then Mrs. Snyder grounded her and left."

And that, of course, was my fault.

Max's eyes flashed with anger. "Karen, I don't like your tone or your accusations. I was the one who asked your mother to talk to Mrs. Snyder."

Karen's body vibrated with anger. "Quit calling her that," she shouted. "She's not my mother. And I don't like the way you always take her side." She whirled around and ran from the room, her footsteps on the stairs echoing down the hall.

Max jumped up from his desk to follow her, but I stood and grabbed his arm. "Let her go. Talking to her when she's this upset won't help at all. Give her a couple minutes."

He didn't meet my eyes, and I could tell he didn't want to listen to me.

"Trust me, Max. Just a couple of minutes. While we wait, let's sit in the family room. It's more comfortable."

His breath was rapid, and his eyes still shone bright green, a sure sign he was upset. He didn't say anything, just followed me.

"Rub your shoulders?" I asked before he sat on the couch, knowing that we would be unable to discuss the Russ situation until he had a chance to talk to Karen.

"Please," he said and settled cross-legged at my feet.

I dug my fingers into his shoulders. He took a deep breath and relaxed. That was a good sign. I needed to talk to him about Carey Snook. Maybe Max would help me figure out what Carey was up to.

I told him first about the fake reporter showing up at the house. Max's muscles tensed. Then I mentioned Carey's hair and mustache, describing them in great detail. Max's body became so rigid that his shoulders felt like granite. He pulled away from me, turned his head, and faced me with green eyes that shot sparks.

"Did you tell Detective Scott about this Carey fellow?" he demanded in a loud voice.

The thought hadn't occurred to me. It should have. The fact that I'd neglected something so obvious hurt my pride and made me want to point the finger elsewhere. "I don't want to talk to Detective Scott. He makes me sick."

"What?" Max stared at me.

"He does. My stomach has been upset since I met him." I knew it wasn't the detective. Since I'd cut back on coffee, my stomach felt a lot better. "When I don't see him, I don't get sick."

"That's ridiculous," Max snapped. "You really don't understand why I'm upset, do you?"

I did, but I was having trouble thinking because he'd never spoken to me like that before. Maybe it's unusual, but in six years of marriage, Max had never yelled at me. "I guess you're going to tell me?" I squeaked. I blinked back tears.

"Yes, I am." He jumped to his feet, and his voice bounced off the walls. "Did it ever occur to you that you could be in danger?"

"Well, not really . . ." Then I remembered how I'd felt tonight at Abbie's. "Maybe. Why?"

He pinched the bridge of his nose. "I can't believe you have to ask that."

My breath caught in my chest. I grabbed a pillow and hugged it. "I can't believe you're hollering at me."

"I've never been so worried before." He

ran a hand through his hair and paced the room, breathing hard. Then he stopped and gazed down at me. "I'm sorry. I shouldn't have yelled."

No, he shouldn't have. I stood and tossed the pillow on the couch. "I'm going upstairs."

I tried to make a dramatic, dignified exit, but Max caught my arm.

"Trish, please."

"Let go." I yanked, but he held tight.

"Honey, listen to me."

I stopped but didn't look at him. "I'm listening."

"We don't know why someone tried to break into the house. Jim Bob's murderer is still on the loose. And we have the situation with your brother hanging over us. I don't know how it all fits together."

"So? I told you guys that was Stefanie. She wants in Jim Bob's storage unit."

"You don't know that." He dropped my arm. "Eric told me I needed to keep a close eye on you. It's harder than holding a cat in water. Sometimes —"

"I know exactly what you mean," I yelled and whirled around. All my insecurities rushed in, battering my mind like an emotional hailstorm. "Sometimes you wish you hadn't married me. I'm just a troublesome redneck and out of your league."

"What?" He put his hands on my shoulders. "Why would you say such a thing?"

"It's true, isn't it? I'm not good enough for you. Your mother always insinuates it. And now my brother . . ." I couldn't continue. I felt my lower lip quiver.

"My mother . . ." Max pulled me close. "Honey, please listen to me. I worry about you — a whole lot. I'm worried about everything that's going on right now, but I have never, ever wished that I hadn't married you."

I didn't feel better.

"I'm sorry," he said. "This has been a bad time. I'm not handling it well. Forgive me, please."

"Okay," I said because I had to, not because I was ready to.

We eyed each other with wariness.

Max sighed. "It doesn't feel okay."

I allowed him to hug me; then I left the room. As I passed the foot of the stairs, I saw movement upstairs. Karen was in the hallway. She had a smile on her face.

14

Thursday morning was gray, raining the proverbial cats and dogs. Max had already gotten up. We still hadn't talked much. He'd spent a great deal of time the night before talking to Karen; then he'd stayed in his office until after midnight.

I sat on the edge of the bed in jeans and T-shirt wondering sleepily which of my five pairs of slippers to wear. Along with my purple fuzzies and pink, cross-eyed rabbits, I also had brown leather moccasins, black-and-white cows, and a simple pair of white slip-ons. I was debating between the moccasins and the bunny slippers when the bedroom door burst open, and Max rushed in.

"Trish? Are you awake?"

Obviously. I was sitting up. I frowned at him. His body language didn't bode well. After last night, I still felt on guard around him. "What's wrong?"

"Eric is here, and he needs to talk with you." Max stood in front of me with his hands on his hips. "Trish, did you come straight home last night after you met Lee Ann?"

I felt his anxiety, and my heart thumped. "Yes . . . no. Well, I stopped at Abbie's first, but she wasn't home."

He groaned. "Come on. Get dressed. He's waiting."

"Okay, but first I have to brush my teeth." I went to the bathroom, shut the door, and stood at the sink, staring in the mirror. My hair looked like someone had turned me upside down and used me to mop a floor. My brown eyes were red-rimmed. Not an attractive sight.

"Dad!" I heard Charlie yell. "Did you know there's cop cars outside again?"

"Yes, son, I know. Go eat breakfast."

I looked briefly at the bathroom window, wondering how long it would take to remove the screen and climb down the side of the house. Would Detective Scott chase me, lights flashing and siren blaring? And what would my hoity-toity mother-in-law say when word got around that her crass daughter-in-law was running down the road in her nightgown? I briefly considered that. It might actually be worth the effort.

"Hey, Dad," Tommy's deeper, booming voice came through the door. "What are the cops doing here? Is Mom in trouble again?"

"Would you please see that the little kids eat breakfast?" Max said. "And that everyone gets ready for school?" His voice sounded stressed. "Trish, come on. Eric's waiting."

"Oh, all right, I'm coming." I brushed my teeth then stumbled out of the bathroom. "What does he want?"

"He wants to know where you were last night."

"Why?" I chose my moccasin slippers, which were a whole lot more dignified than the cross-eyed bunnies.

"He didn't say, but I don't imagine it's good."

Max hadn't smiled at me once since bursting into the bedroom, and he had a hard edge that reminded me of our discussion the night before.

As we walked down the stairs, I heard the sound of Charlie's voice. When we drew closer to the living room, I could finally understand him.

". . . out from *Mysterious Disappearances* that a lot of people aren't who we think they are."

Detective Scott stood in the living room,

along with Corporal Fletcher. Both men were watching Charlie with raised brows.

"Even you could really be someone else, Mr. Detective. That's important to know when you're a cop."

"Charlie, go eat breakfast," Max said.

"But Dad, they need to look into these people —"

"Son, didn't your mother tell you we don't want you watching *Mysterious Disappearances* anymore?"

"But, Dad . . . ," he wailed.

My heart went out to him. He was so frustrated. I knew just how he felt.

Max took Charlie's hand to lead him from the room.

"Why are you still so grumpy, Dad?" Charlie asked. He kept jabbering as they walked down the hall. The sound of his voice faded as they went into the kitchen.

"Charlie reminds me of someone," Detective Scott said thoughtfully, staring after Max and Charlie. Then he squinted in my direction. "You."

An astute observation.

"Why do you need to know where I was last night?" I asked.

The detective glanced at Corporal Fletcher then back at me. "Tell me where you were, please."

Their grim expressions scared me. I sat on the edge of the couch and swallowed hard. "I met Lee Ann at Bo's Burger Barn. We talked for about a half an hour, maybe forty-five minutes. Then I went over to see my friend, Abbie."

"Lee Ann Snyder?" Detective Scott asked.

"Yes," I said.

Corporal Fletcher made a note.

"Abbie Grenville," the detective told the corporal.

He made another note.

"What time did you leave Bo's?" the detective asked.

"I have no idea." The way the two men loomed over me made me feel ganged up on and vulnerable.

"What time did you get to Abbie's?" Corporal Fletcher asked.

"I don't know. I called Max from there. It'll be on our cell phones."

Max came back into the room, forehead wrinkled, cheeks drawn.

"What time did you get home?" Detective Scott asked.

"About ten after nine," Max answered for me.

I waited for the corporal to write that down, which he did. "What is this about?" I asked again.

"We need you to come with us," Detective Scott said. "We have some questions to ask you." He glanced at Max.

He had paled. "Is she being accused of anything?"

The detective shook his head. "I'm not accusing anyone."

Max ran a hand over his head, disheveling his already tousled hair. "I'd better call a lawyer."

"That's your prerogative," Detective Scott said.

I stood, and my legs felt shaky. "Do I really need a lawyer? I mean, is the situation that serious?"

"I can't advise you either way," the detective said. "That's your and Max's decision." He motioned to Corporal Fletcher. "He'll take you to the sheriff's office. I'll meet you there." Detective Scott strode from the room, followed by Max.

I swallowed and glanced at the corporal. "Can I put on some decent clothes?"

"Yeah, Mrs. C., you go on and do that." He was tucking his notepad into his pocket and eyed me. "But don't be long."

Corporal Fletcher showed me into the interview room. The low ceilings and white walls were just as oppressive as they were before.

"I should bring plants to decorate since this appears to be my second home," I grumbled.

"Mrs. C., you need anything?" he asked. "Water?"

I shook my head. "No. I just want to back my life up two weeks and never go shopping at Shopper's Super Saver again." I felt his eyes on me, and I turned to face him. "Corporal Fletcher, this has been the worst two weeks of my life."

He might have had sympathy in his eyes, but Detective Scott walked in, so I didn't have time to find out for sure.

"Mrs. Cunningham, please have a seat." He motioned to my regular chair.

I obeyed. Max had told me to wait for a lawyer, but I just wanted to get the questions over with. Surely nothing could be so bad that I needed legal representation.

Detective Scott sat in his regular chair and placed his arms on the table. Corporal Fletcher remained standing behind him, but he pulled a notebook and pen from his pocket.

Nobody mentioned a lawyer. I had a feeling the cops didn't want me to have one any more than I wanted one.

The detective leaned toward me. "Tell me what you know about Peter Ramsey."

The name sounded familiar. I rubbed my cheeks with my hands. "I don't know. . . . I don't remember."

Detective Scott stared at me. Corporal Fletcher's raised eyebrows indicated that he thought I'd just lied, which wasn't good because, of the two of them, I thought he liked me better.

"You don't know Peter Ramsey?" Detective Scott asked.

"Should I?" I looked at him and frowned. "I know I've heard the name, but I don't remember where. I'm too tired, and I haven't been sleeping well and —"

"We have evidence that you do."

I leaned toward him. "How could you have evidence that I know someone I don't know?"

"Your name and the address of Four Oaks Self-Storage were in his pocket." Detective Scott leaned toward me. "You were seen in an altercation with him."

The light dawned. I recalled why the profile of the man with Stefanie at the dry cleaners had looked so familiar. "Carey Snook. Carey Snook is Peter Ramsey. I knew there was something screwy about him. I mean, that hair said it all, really."

"Carey Snook?" Corporal Fletcher's pen-filled hand was in the air above his note-book.

"Trish, what are you talking about?" Detective Scott asked.

I tapped my fingers on the table. "He told me his name was Carey Snook, and he lied to me about being a reporter at the paper. He's no reporter."

While the two law officers exchanged glances, I wondered how they'd found out about my argument.

The detective turned to me again. "Tell me about Carey Snook."

"Well, besides being an obnoxious liar, he's about your height, big mustache, fake hair. That was the ugliest-looking mess I've ever seen. Sort of like a raccoon. He had funny-looking glasses. Big and black."

"Hmm," the detective said.

I got mad. "*Hmm,* what? I hate it when people *hmm.* Especially you. Don't do that to me."

"Tell me more about Carey Snook," Detective Scott said.

"He's sneaky," I said. "I wanted to yank off his ugly hairpiece."

Corporal Fletcher's pen flew over his note-book.

"And?" Detective Scott stared at me with

his blank expression. He began to tap his pen on the table.

"And what?" I snapped.

Tap, tap, tap, tap.

I wanted to break his pen.

The detective scowled. "And what happened then?"

I couldn't imagine why all this was so important. "He stomped out. Hank, one of our customers . . ." I paused in realization. "That's how you found out about the fight: Hank. He never did like me when he was my teacher. Did you know that he gave me a D in history? I think it was to get even for the time I glued the pages of his teacher's book together. I've never seen anybody —"

"Trish, please answer my question."

Tap, tap, tap, tap.

"Well, Hank accused me of trying to beat Carey up, after which Shirl said it seemed like everything around here was going to you-know-where."

"You-know-where . . . ? Oh." The detective sighed. "Did you threaten him?"

"What? Threaten him? Sure, Detective Scott. I always threaten everyone who irritates me." I jumped to my feet. "If you don't tell me what this is all about, I'm going to leave." I crossed my arms and tightened my lips. "And I won't talk to you again, either."

Before he could answer or argue with me, the door to the interview room opened and a clean-shaven, portly man carrying a very expensive briefcase strolled in. I could tell the gray suit he wore had been made for him. Six years of contact with Max's family had taught me at least that much. And he was so stereotypical of all of Max's father's acquaintances that I knew who he was before he introduced himself.

He placed his briefcase deliberately on the table and gazed at all of us in turn. "I am Calvin Schiller." His smooth, polished voice made me think of a politician. "I'm here to represent Mrs. Cunningham. She will not answer any further questions without my counsel and until I know if you're going to charge her."

I turned around and exchanged glances with Corporal Fletcher. Then I rolled my eyes. I saw the twitch of a smile pass over his lips.

"Mr. Schiller, I don't mind answering their questions." I dropped back into a chair.

He looked down his nose at me, with an expression amazingly like my mother-in-law's. The one that said, *Did I give you permission to speak, redneck peon?* "Mrs. Cunningham, your husband hired me to give you legal advice. At this point in time, I advise you say nothing else."

"But it's no big deal," I said. "All I —"

"Why is she here?" The lawyer stepped between me and the officers, effectively cutting me off.

Detective Scott stood. "Peter Ramsey was found murdered early this morning. It appears that Mrs. Cunningham was one of the last people to be seen with him. Unfortunately, they had an altercation yesterday."

Altercation sounded copish and made me irritable. I jumped to my feet, scooted around Calvin Schiller, and stared at the detective. "So Peter was Carey."

"That might very well be the case," Detective Scott said.

I was mad. Carey Snook had had the nerve to die with my name and number on a piece of paper in his pocket, putting me on another murder-suspect list. I'd also humiliated myself by getting sick in the hallway of the sheriff's office. Then there was my uppity lawyer who treated me like I was a grease stain on his tie. I wanted a lawyer like Andy Griffith's Matlock character. A down-home, country person who ate hot dogs and sang folk songs.

"I don't like Calvin Schiller," I grumbled

at my husband while I sat at the kitchen table, contemplating the toast and jelly on my plate that he'd shoved in front of me. "He's a snob. He probably went to Harvard."

"Well, so did I." Max stood across the table from me. "Calvin is the best lawyer I know. From now on, you don't set foot in the sheriff's office without him."

"I don't want a —"

"I also took the liberty of calling Dr. Starling. You have an appointment with him in two days, right after work. I'll stay with Sammie while you're there."

"You did what?" I clenched my fists. "Does Harvard have classes to teach the students how to be autocratic? So what's next? Are you going to start telling me when to breathe?"

His nostrils flared. "If I feel like I have to, I will."

"Your bossiness is out of control, Max. Besides, I'm feeling better now."

"I'm out of control?" He snorted and crossed his arms.

I glared at him. He glared back. We were in danger of having another fight. Two in as many days would be two too many. I backed off, stuck my finger in the jelly, and then smeared it on the plate like Sammie does.

"We need to talk," Max said.

"Can't talk." I refused to look at him. "I have to eat. That's what you ordered me to do. And we have to go to work, you know."

He ignored what I said. "I'll go get ready while you finish your toast. I'll be back, and then we're going to talk."

He left the room. Reduced to childishness after spending the morning with pushy men, I stuck my tongue out after him. Then I shoved another piece of toast in my mouth. With the interruption of Mr. Harvard Law School at the sheriff's office, I hadn't had the chance to say anything to Detective Scott about Stefanie possibly knowing Peter-Carey, nor had I mentioned that I thought the liar was trying to take over Jim Bob's blackmail business. To me, that meant the two murders might be related. Did I dare call the detective without first contacting my cultured counsel? I was, as my mother would say, between a rock and a hard place. Help Detective Scott or obey my husband? What I really wanted to do was look at my mystery list, but I didn't dare do it right now with Max in this mood.

I washed the crust down with my last gulp of orange juice and wondered who would have killed Peter-Carey and why. Stefanie?

Max appeared in the doorway wearing

jeans and a work shirt. I wasn't ready to forgive him enough to enjoy how he looked.

"You done?" he asked.

My plate was empty. My glass of orange juice was empty. My stomach felt okay.

"No," I said.

He walked into the kitchen and glanced pointedly at the table. "Are you planning to eat the plate?"

"I might get something else." I didn't look at him.

He ignored my words and sat opposite me at the table.

"Detective Scott isn't going to like you anymore," I said. "And you're not winning any popularity contests with me."

Max shrugged. "I'm not trying to be popular. And Eric understands I'm protecting you. He told me to watch out for you when all of this started. And frankly, even if he didn't like me, he isn't my concern. You're all I care about."

I was glad Max cared for me, but I didn't like the way he was showing it. I'd never seen him this controlling. Then again, I'd never before been interviewed by the police about two different murders.

"I didn't kill him, just like I didn't kill Jim Bob. Why do all these people die and point the finger at me?" I looked up at him. "If

I'm a suspect, do you think this means I won't be able to teach Sunday school anymore? I love my Sunday school class."

Max shrugged and shook his head. "I don't know why that would happen unless a parent complains or something. I'm going to call the pastor anyway in the next few days. I'll talk to him about it. The problem is, I don't know exactly how you fit into all of this. I think Peter's death was set up to look like you did it."

I tapped my fingers on the table. "That makes no sense at all. Like I'm that important?"

Max's jaw tensed. "Trish, you're the one who said that you're involved in all of this up to your eyeteeth. I agree. Do you recall the conversation we had last night?"

I stared at my plate. "The one where you yelled at me?"

He reached for my hand, and I reluctantly let him take it. "I'm sorry for that, but yes, that one. Listen, Trish, from what Calvin said, the sheriff's office thinks the two murders are related."

My suspicions were confirmed. I opened my mouth and took a breath to ask for details.

Max held up his hand. "Calvin doesn't know anything for sure. That's just his gut feeling. He also doesn't think you're top on the list of suspects."

I shifted in my chair. If Stefanie did indeed know Peter-Carey, then maybe she did it. I had to get my notebook out and study my clues. I also needed to investigate more.

"Honey?" Max leaned forward, eyes full of concern. "Listen to me. You found Jim Bob. For some reason, Peter wanted to talk with you. Then someone attempted to break into our house. Peter came to see you again, after which he was found dead with your name and phone number in his pocket. Not to mention this thing with Russ and the road sign. There are too many unanswered questions in which you are an active participant."

I stared at Max but didn't see him. Spelled out like that, it sounded really bad for me.

15

My mind whirled with thoughts I itched to write down on my list, but I had no time. Things at Four Oaks Self-Storage were crazy. And that afternoon after work, I was doing chauffeur duties, picking up Karen from the library and Charlie from Mike's.

I guided my SUV up the drive between the library and the woods that bordered the other side. Picnic tables under the tall trees of the lawn reminded me of summers past when I would bring the kids here for reading hour. After that, we'd eat lunch in the shade. I felt a rush of nostalgia that too quickly my kids were growing up. When I was young, I'd dreamed of having a huge family, but then I found out I couldn't. I was grateful I married a man who already had children. Sammie had been my only baby.

Charlie was two when I married Max. Karen had been nine, and Tommy eleven. They weren't too young to feel grief over the loss of their mother. I'm convinced that the loss of a parent, especially at such a young age, leaves lifelong scars that only God can mend.

From age ten to fourteen, Karen had been happier. Although she'd never been cheery like Sammie, she'd been quietly content with her head stuck in a book or listening to music. Our best times were when we read together. That's why I couldn't let Max take her library privileges away, even though I suspected she used the time to meet Julie.

Karen walked from the building, climbed into the car, and said nothing, just slouched in her seat and stared out the window.

I faced her. "Did you have a good time?"

She turned and glared at me. "Why would you care?"

Her tone and words burned me like fire. Perhaps the time had come to prod her and give her an avenue to vent her hostilities. That was the only way I knew to really find out what was wrong.

"Why do I care?" I murmured. "Well now, there's a good question. Probably because I love you. And whether you like it or not, I'm your stepmother and will remain so."

I'd said the stepmother thing on purpose, knowing she would explode. I braced for the blow, asking God to help me.

Her eyes turned to slits, and a red flush crawled up her cheeks. "You're not my real mother," she screamed. "I hate you. The day Dad married you was the second worst day of my life."

I turned away quickly to hide the tears that filled my eyes. She'd aimed to wound me, and it worked.

After I regained control, I faced her. "I'm not your real mother, but I've always loved you as though I were."

She clenched her fists. "Well, you embarrass me. Always hanging all over Dad. Kissing him and stuff. Is that all you guys think about?"

Hurt and anger threatened to choke me. "No. But you need to remember that your father is my husband. That's what married people do." I paused for a breath. "Is that all that's bothering you?"

She slammed her fist on a book in her lap. "No." Her chin quivered. "You're always doing something to get Dad's attention. Like this morning. All those police there. It's so embarrassing. And now you're a suspect. Isn't that just great? My stepmother, the killer. The woman who smashes people to death. How am I going to live that down?" Tears rolled down her cheeks.

I was right. She was jealous. I understood to a degree, but I'd never lost a mother. I also knew that I couldn't deal with this problem myself, nor would it be taken care of by simple conversation. It was bigger than me or Max. God needed to intervene, and perhaps we needed to get some help.

I wished I could cry or scream back at her. Her words cut me as deeply as she'd intended. I felt as though someone had just taken a knife to my heart and sliced it into tiny slivers. But one of us had to be an adult, and since I was older and supposedly more mature, that would be me. I breathed a quick prayer for wisdom.

"Do you think I'm a killer?" I asked softly.

Her anger must have run its course because her body sort of folded in on itself. "No." Then she jerked around to face me. "I suppose you're gonna tell Dad about this?"

"I don't know," I said.

Her hostile silence remained as I picked up Charlie, but letting off steam had helped some. He hopped into the backseat, mouth already in gear. "Mom, you wouldn't believe what Mike has." He picked up an bungee cord from the floor and held it in his hands, stretching it in the air.

"Put your seat belt on," I ordered.

"Mike doesn't have to wear his in the backseat," Charlie said, bouncing up and down.

"Tough. It's the law," I said.

He wiggled around then snapped the buckle. "Mike has a snake. A pine snake. It's not as cool as a boa, but it's still cool." He wiggled the cord, aiming for Karen's head, and hissed.

She swiped his hand away. "Stop it, you moron."

"Karen, don't call him a moron. Charlie, don't tease your sister." I glanced at him in the rearview mirror.

I fought a bone-deep weariness unlike anything I could remember. I took the back way home, deciding no traffic lights were better than the four through town. A mile into our trip, I noticed a beige car behind us. It sped up and then slowed down, moving closer and backing off. A kid, I thought, as I deliberately lowered my speed so whoever it was would pass me.

That didn't work. The vehicle slowed and began to keep steady with my pace. I looked more carefully in the rearview mirror, remembering how I'd been tailgated the night before. I shook my head. Not possible. I was just paranoid.

The car stayed behind me for a mile. My

uneasiness mounted. Then, on a long, straight stretch of road, it leaped forward. My heart pounded. I was afraid I was going to be rammed from the rear, but that didn't happen. It passed me. Too close, and I swerved aside, so it wouldn't sideswipe me. I was too busy controlling my SUV to try to see the driver, but the car was one of those big, old station wagons with fake wood trim on the side. As it roared on down the road, gravel flew from its tires, leaving a pockmark on my windshield.

When we got home, Karen stomped into the house, followed by Charlie, who was still babbling about snakes. I stayed out in the garage and examined my windshield. The hole was large enough that I'd have to get it repaired or cracks would spiderweb all over the glass.

The door opened behind me. I glanced over my shoulder. Max was standing in the doorway, wearing worn blue jeans, a faded blue T-shirt, and a dark scowl. "Karen said you nearly ran off the road?"

She appeared to have a new strategy — trying to make Max think badly of me. Not that that would be hard at this point. "No, I didn't almost run off the road," I stated calmly, ignoring my desire to yell. "Some car passed me too close, and I swerved to get away from it. The tires spit gravel up and left this hole in my windshield. Stupid people. That's the second time I've been tailgated." I poked at the hole with my finger. "I'll call those windshield-repair people tomorrow and see when they can come out."

"What did you just say?" he asked very softly and forcefully.

I glanced around at him in surprise. "I said I would call the windshield-repair people to come out —"

"That's not what I mean." He padded on bare feet over to me, looking tall and formidable. "What did you say about the tailgating?"

I looked up at him. "Tailgating?"

"Yes." He was breathing hard.

I frowned. "Just that I've been tailgated twice."

He ran his fingers through his hair, closed his eyes, and slowed his breathing. "Why didn't you tell me about this right away?"

"Because . . ." I hesitated. "You think it was something to do with the murders, don't you?"

"You don't?" he snapped. "You're the one with lists of clues and suspects. Why wouldn't this occur to you?"

I crossed my arms. "Well, maybe because

Karen had just finished telling me that she hated me. She also said the day I married you was the second worst day of her life."

Max slumped like I'd hit him. "Oh, baby. I'm sorry."

I turned away from him, put my head in my hands, and cried.

Karen pitched a fit worthy of a two-year-old on Friday morning. That was because Max had grounded her from the phone and the library for two weeks, in addition to her other grounding. She was angry with me, of course, because I'd told him what she said.

I was extremely tired, having slept only fitfully. Karen's words kept racing through my mind, as did the fact that I could be in danger, in turn endangering my children. I was also worried about Max. He wasn't coping well. I'd never seen him like this. He might be bossy and a bit arrogant, but he had always been steady. The night before, he'd stayed in his office until the wee hours of the morning. The only good thing was that I'd noticed his Bible open on his desk.

We'd never had this kind of distance between us, and I felt like I was missing a vital organ. I kept praying, hoping for inspiration. I even got up extra early to make waffles because Max loves them, but they had no effect on him. He ate quickly, excused himself, and went into his home office to use the phone. Afterward, he kissed me good-bye and left earlier than normal.

Then Corporal Fletcher came to the door as Sammie and Charlie ran up the stairs to get ready for school.

"Mrs. C., you mind stepping outside?"

I obeyed, too tired to do otherwise. "What did I do now? Are you going to escort me to the sheriff's office again?"

The corporal smiled. "Nope. Sarge told me to come by and talk to you about some car."

"You mean the one tailgating me?" Max must have called Detective Scott.

Corporal Fletcher nodded and pulled his pen and notebook from his pocket. "Tell me everything."

I did, and I gave him the best description I could, given that I hadn't seen much.

When I was done, he put his pen and notebook in his pocket and took a deep breath. "I gotta tell you, I don't like this. I want you to be careful, okay?"

"You sound like Max," I said.

The corporal looked down at me, frowning. "Sarge says you been investigating."

I nodded. "I have to find out what happened." I looked over my shoulder to make sure one of my kids hadn't opened the door. Then I lowered my voice. "Maybe you don't understand, Corporal, but there's a lot at stake here. If my brother is guilty of causing Lindsey's death, my stepkids might never forgive me or Russ. So, I'm asking questions, but only from people I know. It's not like I'm out there with the scum of the earth."

He shook his head. "Mrs. C., you need to stop. Scum doesn't always look like scum. Sometimes they look just like us."

I stared up at him.

He tipped his hat at me, turned, and walked down the stairs. As I watched him go to his car, I shivered.

At Four Oaks Self-Storage, Max's car wasn't in the parking lot. I asked Shirl where he was, but she didn't know. She kept to herself, but her little furtive glances in my direction told me she felt my tension.

I didn't bother calling Max's cell phone. I was too tired. He'd come in when he was good and ready. Bleary-eyed, I put my chin in my hand and stared at my computer screen, but I couldn't focus. The clacking of Shirl's keyboard was punctuated by the occasional ringing of the phone. I closed my eyes and must have drifted to sleep because the sound of Max's voice made me jump.

"Trish?"

I jerked my head up and saw him standing in the doorway.

"Are you sleeping, honey?" He walked in and shut the door behind him.

"Probably." Max had a different air about him. The furrows in his forehead weren't as deep.

He came over and kissed my forehead. "Mind if I sit? I need to talk to you."

"Sure." I waved at a chair, hoping I wasn't in for another lecture.

He pulled it to the front of my desk and sat down, leaning his elbows on the wood top. "I've been to see the pastor."

I sat up straight. "Why?" Was my biggest fear about to come true? Was Max thinking about leaving me? Tears of panic filled my eyes.

He saw my reaction and grabbed both my hands. "Hey, it's okay. I just needed to talk to him."

"What about?" I sought assurance in Max's gaze and found it. He wasn't upset.

"The pastor helped us so much during premarital counseling. I thought maybe he could give me guidance now." Max took a deep breath. "Especially about the Russ thing. I have to tell you, that bothers me a lot."

"I'm sorry," I whispered. "If you only knew how guilty I feel about it. What if the only reason I have you is . . ." My voice broke, and I started to cry.

He stood, walked around the desk, and pulled me to my feet. "I might still be struggling with that, but it has nothing to do with you. And I'll work through it. What's important is that you're my wife and I love you."

I hiccupped.

He rubbed my back. "The other thing that bothers me is that you didn't trust me enough to tell me. Why?"

"I don't know," I said. "I guess I was afraid of your reaction, and I wanted to find out if Russ really did it before I said anything."

He stroked my cheek. "I might be overbearing sometimes, but have I ever treated you badly? Well, except for the other night?"

"Noo, but . . ." A wisp of a thought hit me.

"Honey, this was serious. A man was blackmailing you. I'm your husband. You should have told me."

My thought gelled. "I think it was because of my mother."

Max let go of me and backed up. "What?"

"I avoid confiding in her because she always uses it against me. I guess when this came up, I automatically treated you the same way as I do her."

Max nodded. "I can see that, but I'm not like your mother."

"I know. I'm sorry." I looked up at him. "What did the pastor say?"

"Lots of things," Max said. "Including that you, Karen, and I need to make an appointment to see him together. But that wasn't what we talked most about. He pointed out that I still have an issue with control, which is harder because you're unalterably curious, spontaneous, stubborn, and seem destined for trouble." He gave me a quirky little grin. "I did know that when I married you, by the way. Your father warned me many times."

"He did?"

Max nodded. "For some crazy reason, it's all part of your charm. I wouldn't change any of it. I just need to learn to . . . Well, I can't change you. I can change me. I'm my biggest problem."

I couldn't imagine what he was talking about. "Max, none of what's been happening is your fault. Well, except when you yelled at me and hired that lawyer."

Max laughed. "I know it's not my fault." He squeezed my fingers. "But the way I handle my reaction to everything is my responsibility, and I'm not doing a good job." He sighed. "See, my parents taught me that anything can be taken care of with money or sheer force of will. That eliminates faith from the equation."

"But you're so strong. . . ." I stroked his hand with my thumb.

"Exactly. In myself. And what happens when I'm no longer able to keep a tight handle on things? Am I going to yell at everyone around me? Or am I going to turn to God?" He smiled. "Another thing I've realized is that you and I need time alone. Really alone. Yes, the kids are older, and we've got more freedom, for which I'm glad, but we need to go somewhere. Just you and me."

God had answered my pleas, and so quickly. I stared into Max's eyes, anticipation waking me up. That sounded like an excellent plan. Then I remembered that either Russ or I, possibly even both, might be arrested. I didn't want anything to interfere with time alone with Max. I had to solve this mystery as quickly as possible.

I smacked Daryl with a door in my hurry to get into the building to make my doctor's appointment on time.

"Oh. Sorry. Hi." I looked up at him. I'd

have to be late. I didn't want to miss a chance to ask some questions. I thought about Corporal Fletcher's comment about scum, but I just couldn't see Daryl as a bad guy.

"Hey, Trish." He met my gaze.

"Is your thumb okay?" I asked.

"Uh, yeah." He shifted from foot to foot.

"Listen, Daryl, do you remember that our brothers were friends?"

His lips tightened, and he didn't meet my eyes. "I don't remember a lot. Too painful. Always living in the shadow of a dead younger brother. My mom never recovered."

"I'm sorry." I shifted my purse. "Have you gone to the sheriff's office a lot to be questioned?"

He glanced down at me. "Maybe a couple of times. Like everyone else. Listen, I gotta run. I'm, uh, temporary manager."

"That's great," I said.

He smiled briefly. Then he turned and left.

Well, that didn't get me anywhere but more frustrated. I took a deep breath and went inside.

A couple of minutes later, I was sitting on an examining table.

White coat flapping, Dr. Bill Starling walked through the door of the examining room, holding my folder in his hand. "Trish, how is that stomach?"

"It's okay. Better, in fact. It was just coffee and stress." I wanted to get my appointment out of the way and move on. I had a lot to think about.

He pulled out his stethoscope. "Well, we can take care of you. Let's see what's going on."

Twenty minutes later, minus several vials of blood and other bodily fluids and holding a referral to a gastric specialist, I paid my bill and left the clinic. Bill promised to call me if the blood tests indicated anything that he could help with.

Max had phoned me on my cell to say that he'd returned to the office. George was coming by. Tommy and Karen were home with the little kids.

I decided, spur of the moment, to surprise Max with a picnic dinner. We needed some time to talk. I called Tommy to ask if he'd continue to watch the kids. He grumbled but agreed. I didn't dare ask Karen right now.

I picked up some food and drove back to Four Oaks Self-Storage. Two vehicles were parked in the lot. One was Max's. The other looked familiar, but it wasn't George's. Odd because office hours were over.

I went inside carrying two bags. "Max? I

brought dinner."

"Hi, baby. I'm in my office."

He sounded too perky and bright.

"Is something wrong?" I walked into the room. That's when I remembered why I'd recognized the car parked outside.

Stefanie was perched on the edge of Max's desk, swinging her shapely legs. Sandals with impossibly high heels dangled from her toes. She looked at me rather like the cat that swallowed the canary. The teeny, black skirt and turquoise shirt she wore left very little to the imagination.

Max was in his chair, leaning back, legs stretched out in front of him, arms behind his head. His lips were turned up in a tiny little smile as if he knew exactly what I was thinking.

"Hi, honey," he said.

"Anyone hungry?" I used my iciest tone.

"I'm starving," Max said as if nothing were wrong.

I tossed my purse on the floor, ignoring everything that fell out. I proceeded to place the food and drinks on a file cabinet, laying everything out neatly, giving myself a chance to collect my thoughts. Then I turned around to survey the scene. Max looked disheveled. That was normal and didn't really mean anything. By the end of the day, when he was working on the new part of the facility, he was always tousled.

But the lipstick on the shoulder of his shirt wasn't normal. It wasn't my shade.

I knew that Max wasn't guilty of anything, but Stefanie's motivations . . . Her big, blue eyes took in every move I made, including my reaction when I'd seen the lipstick. I clenched my fists. Her smug expression almost pushed me over the edge. I eyed her precarious position. Just a little shove was all it would take. I could make it appear like an accident, perhaps falling over an imaginary lump in the carpet and bumping into her. Oops. Sorry, Miss Fancy-Pants. Hope you're not hurt — too bad.

"I guess you're wondering why I'm here," she said in her breathy tone.

"No, not really." I met her gaze with a slight smile and can only assume that my thoughts showed in my eyes. For the first time since I'd arrived, she looked worried. "I know exactly why you're here." I didn't look at Max, just kept my gaze focused on her. "You want to get into your dearly departed's storage unit. Did you bring your court order?" I moved closer to her.

"Trish, honey." Max could probably read my mind, and it scared him. "Stefanie is about to leave."

"Yes, she is," I said firmly. I smiled again and moved closer still. Steffie wasn't dense. She hopped from the desk in an unladylike hurry.

"Yes, I'm leaving. And no, I don't have a court order. I — I —" She pouted, and tears welled up in her eyes. "You just don't know how painful this is."

If she thought her tears would move me, she was greatly mistaken. "Oh, I see how it is, all right. Those mean ole court people. Jim Bob has been dead for, what? A little over a week now? Having the right priorities is, after all, a matter of great pain."

Steffie's tears dried up quicker than a drop of water on a hot griddle. She picked up her purse, flung it over her shoulder, and turned to Max.

"Thank you for your sympathy, Maxwell. We'll talk again soon, I hope."

When she turned back to me, I stepped aside for her to leave, motioning toward the front door. "There will be no more talking until you have your court order. Good-bye, Stefanie."

She stomped from the room and the building, slamming the front door behind her. I followed and waited until she pulled from the lot. Then I locked the door and returned to Max's office.

He had his feet up, leaning back in his chair, looking too composed and self-satisfied. That was so like him, I had to try hard not to smile.

"Trish," he said with a little grin.

"Max."

"Baby."

"Don't 'Baby' me." I walked to his desk, placed my palms on the fine wood finish, and leaned over it. "After our nice little talk this morning, I bring you a picnic dinner and interrupt some sort of rendezvous —"

"It wasn't a rendezvous." Max didn't look the least bit repentant.

I stood up straight and crossed my arms. "Then explain the lipstick on your shoulder."

"What lipstick?" He sat up and pulled out the fabric of his shirt so he could see it. The dumb male expression on his face was funny, and I had trouble not laughing. "Well, I'll be," he said in amazement.

"I'll tell you what you'll be — sorry — if you don't explain really fast." I pretended to glare at him.

Max looked at me with a grin. "I love it when you get possessive."

"Don't flatter me. Explain," I ordered.

"Stefanie arrived a little bit ago, right after George left. I was outside doing some last-minute things when she drove up. I managed to call Tommy as she waltzed from her car and begged him to find you and tell you to drive over here. He said you were already on your way. I didn't want to take any chances, which was obviously a wise move. She flung herself at me presumably for a comfort hug."

I wanted to spit nails at the thought of her in my husband's arms. "Comfort?"

He had the nerve to laugh. "After I pried myself loose, I invited her into my office to talk, positioning myself behind my desk and in full view of the security camera." He motioned toward said camera with his head. "I thought about pushing the alarm button under my desk, but I figured I wouldn't do that unless she jumped me. When she heard you come in, she hopped on the desk, posed to give you the full effect of her, ah, assets. I'm not stupid."

I didn't like the fact that he'd even noticed her assets. "All men are stupid," I snapped. "At least when it comes to women's wiles."

He stood and stretched. "Maybe. But, Trish, I love you. I would never do anything like that. If for no other reason than I wouldn't want to be on the receiving end of your temper." He paused. "Is it safe for me to move now?"

"Is that the only reason you wouldn't do anything? You're afraid of my temper?"

"Oh, I think you know better than that." Max walked around the desk.

I pointed at his shirt. "Take that off."

He laughed again and began to undo the buttons. "This is just an excuse to see me in my undershirt."

"You're pretty full of yourself, mister," I said. "I wouldn't push me too far if I were you."

"Oh, don't worry. I remember you used to help neuter your father's cattle."

"I haven't forgotten how," I said.

Max tossed his shirt on the desk. He looked good in his undershirt. All things considered, I felt sorrier for Stefanie than angry. After all, Max was mine.

"You know what?" He reached out for my hand.

"What?"

"I think we should pack up the picnic dinner, put it in the refrigerator here for Shirl and Kevin, and go out. That little French place you love. Just you and me. Alone."

"The one with candlelight and servers in tuxes?" I asked.

He smiled. "Yep."

"And we can hold hands under the table and stare into each other's eyes over the table?" I was getting excited.

He grinned and nodded.

"Then we can share a dessert and you can feed me from your fork?" I could barely contain myself.

"If that's what you want."

I thought the idea was brilliant.

16

On Saturday morning, the house was quiet. My spur-of-the-moment date with Max the night before had been as romantic as I'd hoped, more than making up for the days I felt so guilty and bereft. He knew how to sweep me off my feet, and he'd done it with abandon, leaving me feeling breathless. The only rough moment had been when he informed me he was going to hire a PI to help solve the question of Russ. I was mildly offended that he didn't think I was capable of discovering the truth, but more than that, I was afraid where the truth might lead.

However, I was so happy to have our relationship back on an even keel I let the topic go. Today, Tommy was out with friends. Max took the other kids to the mall and then to lunch at Bo's before the playoff game. I had suggested the outing and stayed home in an effort to give the children time alone with him. I hoped Karen would come around and realize that she was as important to him as I was. Perhaps doing this on a regular basis would alleviate possible future problems with our younger kids.

They would be heading to the game immediately after lunch. I was going to eat with Abbie and then join my family at the ball field.

I made lasagna for Sunday. Then, while I waited to leave, I settled in the family room, holding my steno pad. Several things besides Stefanie's visit to Max spurred me on to think about my mystery. Knowing I was in danger, for one, and in turn, so were my children. But now I had the additional challenge of beating a PI to an answer, if I could.

I flipped the pad open and added the fact that Peggy Nichols had been dragged to the sheriff's office for questioning. Then I reviewed the notes I'd already written down.

Stefanie. Why did she want in Jim Bob's storage unit? I bit my lip, and a thought occurred to me. If Jim Bob was blackmailing everyone else, maybe he held something over Stefanie's head, too. Why else would she stay with him? I jotted down: *Was Jim Bob blackmailing Stefanie? What's in the unit that she wants so bad?*

I looked at my next note. *Frank — embezzling; Jim Bob — blackmailing?* Why was

Frank so hostile? I scribbled: *Frank is weird and creepy. Makes me scared.*

Now, what about Daryl? I'd already written, *Daryl sleeping with Stefanie?* What else did I know about him? I tapped the pen against my head. Then I wrote: *Did his brother take the road sign?* I also added: *smashed thumb and stitches,* although I couldn't figure out how that fit in.

Then there was Lee Ann. I knew she was upset about Norm. But how could that have led to her killing Jim Bob? Besides, she was a woman. Jim Bob might have been middle-aged, but he was still a man and wouldn't have lain down and let her stab him. That had to have taken strength.

And that led me to the question I'd forgotten about. Why wasn't there blood all over the milk case? Unless Jim Bob had been stabbed somewhere else and moved. That was possible given he was on the cart.

As I wrote that down, the phone rang. I took my notebook to the kitchen and yanked the receiver off the wall.

"Hello?"

"Trish? This is Bill — Dr. Starling."

"Hi, Bill."

"Tried to reach the cell phone number you gave me, but no one answered."

I stuffed my notebook into the kitchen

junk drawer to hide it and grabbed my purse to see if I'd lost my phone again.

"What can I do for you?" I asked as I dumped the contents on the kitchen table. I couldn't imagine why he'd call me at home on a Saturday.

Bill cleared his throat. "Well, last minute I decided to do an additional test. I was in the office for an emergency this morning and noticed the results. If you made that appointment with the specialist, you can cancel it."

"Why?" I still couldn't find my phone and headed for the garage to look in the SUV.

"Remember when you were pregnant with Sammie? How coffee made you sick? I took the liberty of doing a pregnancy test just to eliminate that possibility. I'm glad I did. You're pregnant. Congratulations."

I stopped midstep, feeling as though I'd been hit in the stomach. All my thoughts crashed and jumbled into a useless wad of incoherence.

"Trish? Are you there?"

"Yeah," I managed to say. How could I be pregnant?

"You should make an appointment with an obstetrician as soon as possible, given your background. You'll be able to get help with the nausea if it's still a problem. And then you'll find out how far along you are."

"Bill, I can't be pregnant. You know that. All the doctors said I couldn't conceive again. Besides, I'm thirty-two."

"Still a perfect age to have a baby. And you did have Sammie despite the odds. Sometimes miracles happen. You really need to stay out of trouble now. You've got a baby to think about."

"I've had coffee to drink and two painkillers." Like that was my biggest concern.

"Not to worry. Just stop. Call me if I can do anything else for you." He hung up.

I held the receiver in my hand. *Pregnant?* Worry overran a tiny quiver of happiness. Max and I had tried for two years to have another baby after Sammie, but the doctors said it was highly unlikely unless we sought very expensive procedures. Neither of us felt right about that and agreed that four children were enough. I knew Max didn't really want any more kids at his age. I still did but had to agree that four were plenty. How many times recently had he insinuated that he was glad they were all getting older? Last night at the restaurant, he'd mentioned how happy he was that we were going to have more time together because the kids were growing up. How would I tell him this news? Especially on top of everything else.

I glanced at the clock. I was due over at Abbie's. The way things were planned, I could avoid telling Max until after the game. If he saw me beforehand, he'd know something was up. Even though he'd come to terms with things recently, I didn't want to add to his burden, especially right before a game. He might be upset, play horribly, lose, and I'd feel doubly guilty. Besides, I needed some time to sort this out. With Abbie.

My cell phone was nowhere to be found. As I dressed to go out, I tried to recall where I'd put it. The last time I'd used it was to call Tommy and tell him I was going to see Max. It had been in my purse then, and . . . it must have fallen out in Max's office.

I called Four Oaks Self-Storage and asked Kevin to look for it. As I suspected, it lay under one of Max's chairs. I asked Kevin to put it on Max's desk and said I'd be there to get it in a couple of hours.

Abbie met me at her door with a hug. "Come on into the kitchen. I'm finishing our lunch." I followed her and sat at the breakfast bar. She went back to the counter where she was working. "You going to the game after we eat?"

I nodded. "First I have to go get my phone

from the self-storage. It fell out of my purse in Max's office."

She glanced over her shoulder at me and laughed. "You and your phone. You should attach it to your purse with rope. Hey, you want coffee? I can make some."

"I can't. It makes me sick when I'm pregnant."

"What?" She turned around, bread in one hand, knife in another. "How far along?"

"I don't know. Bill told me an hour ago."

"Wow." She grinned. "Well, given the past and the fact that all the doctors said this wasn't likely to happen, I guess it's a miracle."

That was what Bill had said. Would Max see it the same way?

"I guess you're right." I rubbed my fingers over the beige countertop.

"You haven't told Max yet, I take it?" she asked.

"No. I don't want to tell him until after the game." I paused. "Truthfully, I don't want to tell him at all. Lately he's been talking a lot about how glad he is that the kids are getting older."

She smiled. "I think he'll be happy."

"I don't know." I shifted on my stool.

"Let's eat in the living room," she said. "It'll be more comfortable."

She handed me two plates to carry. I hopped off the stool and ambled into the living room to wait for her, relaxing in her eclectic taste. Framed modern art accented the red wall above the sofa. The rest of the walls were off-white. Her desk was in an alcove on one side of the room. Shelves, where she kept all her reference books, covered the three walls. I'd never really taken an in-depth interest in her research before, but now, as I looked over the bindings, I realized I'd been stupid. Given that many of the books were about cops and forensics, Abbie could probably answer my question about Jim Bob's lack of blood.

Distracted from my immediate concern over the pregnancy, I put the plates on the glass coffee table and went over to the shelves. I pulled out a book called *Crime Scene Investigation* and riffled through the pages.

Ice tinkled behind me as Abbie walked into the room. "What are you looking at, hon?"

I turned with the book in my hand. "Jim Bob was stabbed, but there wasn't any blood splattered anywhere. Why? Besides the fact that maybe he'd been moved?"

Abbie put the glasses on the coffee table. She then came over to where I stood. "Two reasons as far as I know." She took the book from me, flipped through the pages, and pointed. "One is that he was on his back and was stabbed in the liver. That would result in internal bleeding."

I glanced at the page. That was possible given Jim Bob's position and where the knife had been located. I looked up at her. "What's the other reason?"

"He was already dead when he was stabbed."

When I arrived at Four Oaks Self-Storage, the door was unlocked, but Kevin wasn't at the front desk. His car was in the parking lot, along with another that I didn't recognize. I wondered if he'd gone out to show someone a unit.

I ran into Max's office, but my phone wasn't on the desk. I heard a step behind me.

"Kevin?" I asked, looking under some papers. "Where is my phone?"

No one answered. I turned around to see the muzzle of a gun in my face. My breath caught in my throat like a choke hold.

"Lose this?" Stefanie Jenkins asked, grinning widely and holding my phone in her hand.

After I started breathing again, I realized

my phone wasn't the only thing that had been lost. She no longer had an accent. And for once, she'd dressed like a normal person in blue jeans and a cotton shirt that covered everything.

"It's so convenient that you're here," she said.

"Where is Kevin?" I hoped maybe he'd been out of the building when she arrived and he'd come in and rescue me.

"He's, shall we say, indisposed in the back room closet." She smiled slowly. "It's amazing what most men will do when a pretty girl offers them favors. He was so easily overcome."

She tossed my phone on the floor and pressed the gun into my stomach, making me wince. Then she pulled two keys from her pocket and dangled them from perfectly manicured fingers. "I'm quite convincing. Kevin confessed to me that the unit was double locked. He also gave me the code to get into the building. I don't need you, but you're coming with me anyway."

"What happened to your accent?" I asked.

"I'm not from the South at all." She jabbed the gun harder. "Come on."

I really had no choice seeing as how she had a weapon pointed at me. Then I remembered the alarm button and sidled toward

Max's desk.

"You must really think I'm a moron, Trish. Touch that alarm, and your guts are going to be splattered all over this office."

I did what she asked. Guts all over the place proved too vivid a description to ignore.

With her gun in my back, we walked to the climate-controlled building that housed Jim Bob's unit. I wished that one of our customers would pull in right now, but no one did. Saturday afternoons could be very slow. I punched the code into the keypad to get inside. The twenty-minute light came on, illuminating the hallway and the insides of the units. She handed me the keys. I undid the padlocks and pulled up the door.

People often keep weird things in their storage units, from cookies to trash, but I'd never seen the likes of Jim Bob's. It looked like a home office, complete with a desk, swivel chair, battery-operated light, and three large file cabinets.

Stefanie shoved me inside. I fell to my knees and bashed my head on the corner of the desk. Blood began to dribble down my face. I tried to stop the bleeding with pressure while I watched her, just wishing for one chance to pull her hair out by the roots. Why hadn't I knocked her off Max's desk when I had the chance?

She shut the unit door and turned. "Do you know what my biggest regret is?"

I shook my head.

She closed her eyes and sighed. "That I didn't get a piece of that husband of yours. I certainly tried hard enough and on many different occasions."

Pulling her hair out by the roots wasn't going to be enough.

Her eyes shot open. "I should kill you just because he was faithful. Most men eventually succumb, even if it's just once. Maxwell never did."

My husband had never mentioned the other times she'd tried to seduce him. That made me so mad I stood up and took two steps toward her without thinking.

"Stop right there. Don't do that again. I'll pull this trigger in a second." She waved the gun at me. "Sit down against the wall and put your hands on top of your head."

I did what she said and looked around the unit. File cabinets, a desk . . . I knew what it all was. "I guess this was Jim Bob's headquarters?"

She nodded. "Yes. My dear husband's second job."

"So," I said, "he was probably blackmailing half of the town."

"Quite a few. He never asked for much from anyone. Just a little money or other things here and there. Didn't seem like much, taken one at a time, but altogether it was quite lucrative." She pulled a drawer from the desk.

"Did you kill him?"

"Oh my, no." She'd turned on her southern accent again. "Stabbing someone? Sugar, I'd get my nails dirty. If I ever wanted to kill someone, I'd make sure it wasn't messy." On her knees, she reached into the empty hole where the drawer had been and pulled out some keys.

"Do you know who did?" I asked.

"Nope." She got to her feet, smiling. "Lots of people had reason to, including you." She glanced up at me slyly. "Isn't it ironic that you've been hauled down to the sheriff's office on a regular basis?"

"Did you have an affair with Daryl?" I asked.

"Until I found out who held the purse strings at his house." She walked over to a file cabinet.

"Why'd you stay with Jim Bob?"

"Everyone has things to hide. Unfortunately, he made me pay for my secrets by staying with him. Besides, there were other things I wanted." She waved the gun at me again. "Now, shut up, will you?"

She unlocked a file cabinet and yanked open a drawer. Her breath hissed through her teeth. She unlocked another and opened it. Then another. In a frenzy, she jerked every drawer open. One of the cabinets leaned forward. I wished it would fall on top of her and break her legs. She whirled around and faced me.

"Who took everything out of here?" She moved closer, pointing the gun at me. "Did you?"

I shook my head mutely, wondering if I was about to die.

"Did Maxwell?"

"I don't know."

If she shot a bullet at close range, would it travel through my body into the next unit? I remembered the baby. I couldn't die here.

She stomped her feet, cursed, and spun around, wiping the desktop clean with her arm. Everything crashed to the floor. The light broke into two pieces. "It was the police. I'm sure it was."

She stood silently; then she turned to face me again, this time with slow deliberation that was far scarier than her frenzy. "All that time your husband was leading me on, making me think the stuff was still in here."

She moved closer to me and stood very

still. I knew in that moment that she wanted nothing more than to get even with Max by killing me. I closed my eyes and prayed. Tension crackled in the silence. Neither of us moved, though I felt her gaze on me like heat.

The thought of Max finding me dead was more than I could stand. Poor man. He'd be a widower twice. And my baby would die. I wanted to cry, but I was too afraid. Instead, I involuntarily reached up and grabbed the cross necklace Max had given me, thinking about how much he meant to me and how badly I wanted to live and spend the rest of my life with him. She said she wouldn't kill someone in a messy way. *Please, God. Please let her remember that.*

Her breathing changed, and I felt the air shift as she moved. I opened my eyes, expecting to see the barrel of the gun pointed at my head. Instead, she'd walked over to the unit's closed door.

"I'm leaving you locked in here. Everyone is at the baseball game. They'll only start missing you in a couple hours. That'll give me time to get away. I hope they find you before you die of thirst."

With that, she turned her back, walked out of the unit, and pulled the door down, wheels grating in their tracks. Then I heard the snaps of the padlocks shutting. The outside door slammed as she left, sending a *whoosh* of air down the hall that vibrated the building's metal walls. The lights went out, leaving me in total blackness.

17

The building creaked and settled around me. I stood up and wondered when Max would notice I wasn't at the game. My legs started to shake. I groped around until I found Jim Bob's desk chair and dropped into it. Max and Detective Scott were going to kill me if I didn't die in this unit first. I'd done exactly what they told me not to do. Put myself in danger, although I really couldn't have anticipated this.

I heard voices in the distance. They could belong to anyone, so I didn't get my hopes up. Where was Stefanie? She must have gotten a new car, because I didn't recognize the one in the lot as hers.

I thought about how she'd tried to seduce Max over and over again. My shaking stopped. I got mad. How dare Miss Fancy-Pants lock me in a storage unit? I hopped out of the chair and shuffled over to the wall, feeling my way to the door. There had to be a way to break out of here. I'd do it, even if I had to dismantle the door with my bare hands. I'd just begun to investigate the mechanism with my fingers when I heard the building door open. The lights came on.

I held my breath. Had Stefanie changed her mind and returned to shoot me? I reached down and grabbed the body of the broken desk light to hit her with.

"Trish? Are you in there?"

Max. I was so relieved to hear him that I didn't care if he was mad, as long as he hugged me first. I dropped the piece of lamp I held.

"Yes," I said.

The locks jiggled, and then the door slid open revealing Max, Detective Scott, and Corporal Fletcher.

"Thank God." Max rushed in, yanked me into his arms, and held me tight. Very tight. Too tight.

"Max," I gasped.

"What, baby?"

"I can't breathe."

"Oh, sorry." He loosened his grip. Then he noticed the blood and examined my head with his fingers. "Are you hurt bad?"

Corporal Fletcher moved closer to us. "Mrs. C., you need to go to the doctor and get that checked out."

"I'll be okay." I tried to push Max's hand away. All the tall men hovering nearby were making me irritable.

"I'm glad to see you alive," Detective Scott said. "We got Stefanie."

"How did you know I was here?" I asked. "Why didn't I hear sirens?" I wished Max would stop messing with my head.

"Abbie," he said. "I called her when you didn't show up. She told us where you'd gone."

Detective Scott nodded. "We didn't use the sirens because we didn't want to broadcast the fact that we were coming."

Max's arm was securely around my shoulders as we walked from the climate-controlled building. Cop cars with flashing lights surrounded the office, and five or six uniformed deputies stood around. Too many cops.

"Kevin's in the storage closet," I said. "I imagine he'll think twice before kissing another woman again."

Detective Scott glanced at me. "We found him."

I thought about Stefanie trying to seduce Max. My anger grew. "Where is Steffie?"

"In a cruiser," the detective answered.

"I want to see." I pulled away from Max and headed toward the cop cars.

Max hurried to keep up with me. "Trish, I don't think that's a good idea." He realized my true intention. The other men didn't know me so well.

I marched to the car where she was held. I hoped she wasn't handcuffed — that she would jump out and attack me, because I was ready to take her down.

I yanked the door open.

Across the parking lot, one of the deputies who was jaw jacking with another, noticed me. "Ma'am, you can't do that," he yelled.

I heard footsteps running toward me. Stefanie didn't look up.

"Not too brave when you don't have a gun, are you?" I snarled at her. "And who's going to do your nails in jail, anyway? Too bad, because that orange color you wear might match your prison jumpsuit."

She shifted until her back faced me.

"Mrs. C.," Corporal Fletcher said behind me, "you need to get away from the car."

I ignored him, clenching my fists. "I should have shoved you off Max's desk when I had a chance."

The corporal appeared in my field of vision and grasped my arm. I felt Max's hands on my shoulders and realized that as much as I wanted to rip Stefanie's hair out, the loss of dignity wasn't worth it. Not to mention a possible lawsuit, another trip to the sheriff's office, and possible time in jail for assault.

I slammed the car door and turned to face Max. "I want to go home." Then I glared at the detective and Corporal Fletcher. "I absolutely do not want to talk to that advocate person. She's too nice."

The men glanced at each other.

"Fletcher can take a statement right now," Detective Scott said.

For the second time that week, I sat on the edge of an examining table. This time at the hospital emergency room. Max sat in a chair in a corner.

After bandaging my head, the emergency room doctor began to scribble on his pad. "I'm going to write you a prescription for pain medication."

If he did, Max would make me take it, and I couldn't because of the baby. This wasn't exactly the place I wanted to tell him.

"Make sure it's safe for pregnant women," I whispered, hoping Max wouldn't hear me.

The doctor glanced up at me. "Did you say you're expecting?"

Max's head jerked up, and his eyes widened. "Expecting?"

The doctor glanced from me to Max. "Okay, that changes things a little." He tore up the paper he'd already written and started a new one.

"You're pregnant?" Max said, sitting very still.

The doctor eyed Max as he handed me a slip of paper. "Ah, let me know if there's anything else I can do." He hurried from the room.

"You're pregnant?" Max demanded.

"Yes." I didn't look at his eyes, just gazed at his chin.

He stood. "Let's go."

He helped me off the table and pulled the curtain aside to let me pass. I finally glanced at him, but now he wasn't looking at me. I felt the prickle of tears in my eyes but kept them at bay. He guided me out of the building to the car. There, he opened the door for me, holding my arm as I got in. Then he got into his side.

I didn't speak. Max's breathing was irregular, and he tapped a finger on the steering wheel.

"How long have you known?" he asked quietly.

"Since this afternoon." I couldn't think of anything else to say.

We lay silently in bed. We hadn't really talked yet, but that wasn't Max's fault. He'd tried, but I hadn't given him a chance. I felt unreasonably cranky, out of sorts, and mad that he hadn't been ecstatic when he learned about the baby, even though I knew perfectly well that his reaction was predictable given the circumstances. When we got home, I immediately took a shower and went to bed, leaving him to talk to the kids, call my parents, and even call his folks if he wanted to. Someone had to explain my latest mishap, and I wasn't in the mood.

I tossed and turned, and slumber evaded me. When he got into bed, I pretended to be asleep.

Soft light from the street filtered through the blinds. A dog barked in the distance.

Max rolled over. "I know you're awake."

"How?" I asked.

"The way you're breathing. Plus, your fists are clenched."

Stupid fists. They were clenched on top of the covers. I immediately relaxed them and shoved my hands under the blanket, keeping my eyes closed. "Okay, I'm asleep now."

"Come on, Trish. Neither one of us will get any rest if we don't talk."

"Are you going to fuss at me?" I asked with my eyes still shut.

"No."

"Promise?" I peeked at him.

"Yes." He was on his back with his hands under his head and his ankles crossed. "I'm sorry. I know my reaction wasn't what you expected."

"Actually, it was precisely what I expected," I grumbled.

He sat up and turned on the light. Then he stuffed a pillow behind him and leaned against the headboard. "I'll admit, I was upset."

"Duh," I said, sitting up and shoving my pillow behind my head.

He glanced at me. "Not because you're pregnant, but because you hadn't told me, especially after our recent issues. That wasn't exactly a great way to find out."

"It wasn't exactly how I'd planned to tell you," I said, meeting his gaze.

He frowned. "Well, that brings us to the crux of the matter. When were you planning to tell me?"

"After the game," I said.

He looked away from me, focusing on his toes. "I thought we agreed that we would tell each other everything." He paused. "So did you tell Abbie?"

"Yes," I said.

His expression was bland, but his right cheek muscle was twitching. "I'm your husband, Trish. Why didn't you call me and tell me first?"

I sat up and pushed some of his hair back, feeling like the most horrible wife in the world. I'd hurt him. "Oh, honey. I'm sorry. I wasn't thinking, I guess. As usual. I was worried about your reaction. I didn't want you to lose the game, which happened anyway because you guys had to come and rescue me."

"We've rescheduled." He adjusted the pillow under his neck and stared at the wall. "Is that the only reason?"

"I figured you'd think I did it on purpose and be mad. I knew you didn't want more kids. I talked to Abbie first so I could figure out a way to tell you."

He took my hand. "That makes no sense. How could you have done it on purpose? It takes two, doesn't it?"

That was just like Max to say such a logical thing. I faced him. "You're right. I was wrong. What can I do to make up for this?"

He smiled slowly. "First, come here and let me hold you. Second, don't get locked in any more storage units. Third, don't keep anything else from me."

I scooted next to him and put my lips to his ear. "I didn't get locked in that unit on purpose."

"I know." He kissed me. "I love you.

And . . . well, your pregnancy is unexpected and not exactly what we'd planned, but sometimes things happen for a reason. In fact, given all the odds, this baby has to be a gift from God."

"Really?" I wrapped my arm around him.

"Yes, really." He kissed me again.

A bit later, I wasn't sleeping yet, but I was content. We'd discussed baby names and decided to tell the kids the next day. Max was already breathing evenly like he does right before he falls asleep. I was happy to be next to him. I wasn't dead or shivering in Jim Bob's storage unit.

Old Jim Bob, the man everyone hated. So much so that someone killed him. Stefanie denied it, but she was certainly interested in something that he kept in his secret office in one of the file cabinets . . . empty file cabinets . . . I'd forgotten to ask Max about them.

I sat up and turned the light on.

Max jumped up as if on a spring. "Are you okay?" He stared at me with wide eyes.

"Yes, I'm fine. When did the police get the stuff out of Jim Bob's unit, and why didn't you say anything? You had to have let them in. Did they have a search warrant? Did they need one? Furthermore, what was in there that Stefanie wanted so badly? Do you know?"

Max groaned and lay back down, pulling the pillow over his head.

I yanked it off his face. "No sleeping until you tell me."

He kept his eyes shut. "I guess there's no chance this can wait until tomorrow morning?"

"I won't be able to sleep for wondering."

Max sighed, rolled on his side to face me, and rested on his elbow. "Okay. Yes, Eric searched Jim Bob's unit not too long after the murder. Yes, they had a warrant. Yes, I let them in. I don't know exactly what he found, but it must have implicated Stefanie in some way because he was keeping an eye on her. However, he let everyone, including her, think that the unit was intact."

"You knew and didn't tell me?" I demanded.

He sighed. "Yes, I knew. And I didn't tell you."

"And you're mad at me for not telling you things?" I huffed.

He shook his head. "I think the situations are just a little different."

That was beside the point. "So why didn't you tell me?"

"Because Eric asked me not to."

I sat up and crossed my legs. "Is there

something wrong with me? Am I untrustworthy? Did neither of you think I could keep a secret?"

"It wasn't my decision. And I assume he wanted as few people to know as possible. Police business and all. Besides, he was treating you as a suspect."

Max's words didn't pacify me.

"Can I go to sleep now?" he asked.

"No. I'm not done." I crossed my arms. "I know Jim Bob was blackmailing people. What exactly did they find inside? Copies of blackmail letters? And what did Stefanie want in there?"

Max shook his head. "I don't know."

"She's tricky enough to commit murder, but I didn't see her in the grocery store that morning. At least I don't think so. Unless she was in disguise. Do you think she killed him?"

He shrugged one shoulder.

"Who is Stefanie, anyway?" I asked. "You know her southern accent was fake, don't you?"

He said nothing, just kept staring at me.

"Do you know what she told me?" I clenched my fists. "She was sorry she didn't get a piece of you."

Max raised his eyebrow. "And that bothers you?"

I frowned. "Well, yeah, because she said she tried more than once."

He laughed. "You have absolutely nothing to worry about."

I scowled at him. "Besides having the morals of an alley cat, who was she really?"

He groaned. "I don't know. I don't care. I want to sleep."

I shifted positions and bounced. "How can you sleep knowing that you don't know who she really is?"

"Easy. Watch." He reached over me, turned out the light, and flopped back on the bed.

"But —"

"Hush," he said. "Go to sleep."

18

"I — am — so — humiliated!" Karen pushed her chair from the table and jumped up. "I can't believe it, Dad. You're too old to have babies." She ran from the room.

We'd made the big announcement to the kids during a special Italian-themed Sunday lunch. Karen's reaction didn't surprise me at all.

Max put his fork down. "I'll go talk to her."

"No," I said. "Leave her alone. Don't let her ruin the meal for the rest of us."

He took a deep breath, debating his decision. "Okay," he finally said.

Sammie kept eating tiny bites of lasagna noodles and watching everyone. Charlie's mouth was stuffed full of Italian bread.

Tommy grabbed another piece of lasagna. "Don't mind her. Julie is a wreck, so Karen is a wreck. Girls can be so dramatic."

I agreed, although I'd seen my share of

melodramatic men. When Karen became human again, I'd encourage her to join the drama club.

Sammie put her fork down and eyed first her father, then me. "Why?" she asked.

"Why what, sweetie?" I took a bite of salad.

"Why is Daddy too old? What happens with babies?"

Tommy snorted and covered his mouth. Max's lips twitched. I blinked and for a moment couldn't figure out what she meant. Then I got it and blushed. Max and Tommy looked at me as though answering the question was my responsibility.

Was there any way I could deflect this until she was older? "Well, uh, Sammie . . ."

Charlie interrupted me with a wave of his hand. "It's no big deal. In Sunday school this morning, we read about how that Abraham guy had kids when he was really ancient. That means Dad can have them, too."

"Oh," Sammie said. "Okay."

And that took care of that.

Old man, I mouthed at Max.

He winked at me and grabbed my hand.

After lunch, I rewarded Charlie for his quick thinking by agreeing to sit down and watch *Mysterious Disappearances* with him.

I had to admit that by the time the show was half over, I was hooked.

During a commercial break, he turned to me with a wide grin. "This is how I knew that Mrs. Jenkins was a bad lady."

"Huh?" I'd missed something.

"I saw a show about a lady who rips off rich men. She marries them and disappears with all their money."

I gaped at him.

Apparently that was enough encouragement because he began to talk faster. "I tried to tell you, Mom. First I saw a picture of that guy who worked at my school on the show. Then I saw a really bad picture of her. He was her husband, but he was supposed to be dead."

That's why Charlie saw dead people. And everyone thought he was imagining things. Poor kid. "I'm sorry we didn't listen." Things began to fall into place in my mind. I ruffled his hair. Charlie would be getting his own *Mysterious Disappearances* book for his birthday.

I needed to review all my clues. If what Charlie said was true, then Steffie had plenty of motivation to murder Jim Bob. But she wasn't there that day, was she? And where did Peter-Carey fit in? Was he the accomplice? The supposed dead man who was now really dead? She had denied any part of the murders. As much as she'd been bragging, it seemed to me that she would have bragged about that, too.

I'd spread the contents of my kitchen junk drawer on the counter to look for my mystery notebook. It was gone. Perhaps I wasn't remembering right where I'd put it.

Max had taken all the kids out for ice cream, leaving me home to rest. His orders. My short confinement in the storage unit caught up with me after lunch. My head hurt, as did my body, and of course I didn't want to take anything for the pain because of the baby. So I was going to rest as ordered. With my clues. But now I couldn't find the steno pad. As I stuffed everything back into the drawer, the doorbell rang. I slammed the drawer shut and made my way to the front door, aching muscles protesting against my attempt to hurry.

Through the peephole, I saw Detective Scott. I flung the door open. "Why are you here? I didn't do anything."

He smiled. "I know you didn't. I just need to talk to you for a moment."

I stepped back to let him in. "We can go into the family room. Max and the kids are out getting ice cream. I'm supposed to be napping."

Detective Scott followed me. He was dressed casually, in dress pants and shirt, not in a uniform or a suit, but he still made me nervous. I hoped I wouldn't have to call my erstwhile lawyer.

"Have a seat." I motioned to one of the white, overstuffed, slipcovered chairs, and watched him with suspicion.

"I'd like to review your statement from last night." He sat, holding some papers on a clipboard.

I relaxed and dropped onto the sofa. "That's fine."

He talked me through my confrontation with Stefanie, helping me remember things that I'd forgotten about. Because so much had happened in such a short time, I felt as if I was in some emotional netherworld, one step removed from everything.

When we were done, he had me sign the form. Then he sat back down and studied me. His eyes were different than they had been the times he'd interviewed me. Not so pinpointed and hard. "Trish, are you feeling okay?"

"I guess I'm a little numb, at least emotionally. My body aches, and my head hurts. Probably from when Steffie pushed me across the storage unit." As if to confirm my statement, a muscle spasm in my shoulder made me wince.

He leaned forward. "You need to take care of yourself now. You've got a baby to worry about."

"Yeah." I was rubbing my shoulder. But then I stopped. I hadn't told him I was pregnant. "How did you know?"

His face twitched. "Abbie Grenville. She, ah, informed me at church. Then she told me to leave you alone."

I hadn't realized they went to the same church. I wanted to laugh at his expression. Like he'd been chastened. "She looks out for me."

"Obviously," he said.

I folded my legs under me. "We've been best friends since kindergarten."

"That explains a lot," he muttered.

I decided to let that comment go, although I was certain it wasn't complimentary. "I have something to tell you that might be important."

He sat up straight, eyes fastened on my face, becoming a cop once again.

I told him about Charlie and *Mysterious Disappearances.*

"Yes. I checked into that. Your stepson is observant." The detective tapped his finger on his leg. "A good cop follows every lead, even those from a kid."

A lesson I would do well to learn.

I decided to take advantage of Detective Scott's regard for my son's brilliance and tell him what I thought. "I don't believe Stefanie killed two men."

His body tensed, and he squinted at me. "I want you to forget about the whole thing. You don't have to be involved in this anymore."

"Then I guess I'm not a suspect?" I asked.

"I never said you were."

But you sure acted like it. I put my hands on my legs and went back to my original topic as though he hadn't spoken. "I was there with her in that storage unit. She could have killed me. If she were a murderer, she would have. What did she have to lose? I don't think I'm reading this situation wrong."

"You need to stop thinking about it," he said.

"But —" I started to argue; then I saw the expression on his face and understood. He didn't believe the murderer was Stefanie, either. That meant that Jim Bob and Peter-Carey's killer was still on the loose. But why wasn't I still a suspect?

Silence filled the air between us. I met his gaze and ignored his order to stop thinking.

"Here's my biggest question. Why wasn't there blood from Jim Bob's body squirted all over the place in the cold room? Was it because he was on his back and got stabbed in the liver or because he was already dead?"

Detective Scott's breath hissed through his teeth. Poor man. I'd caught him off guard. "Trish, I told you to . . . You're not going to stop thinking about all this, are you?"

I shook my head. "I can't. I also have to figure out about Russ and the stop sign."

"I heard Max hired a PI," Detective Scott said.

"Yes," I grumbled. "Probably some high-falutin, educated, Cunningham-type guy who's too big for his britches. Like that lawyer."

Detective Scott laughed.

I joined him; then I sobered. "I have to know."

"I'm sure it's only a matter of time until the truth comes out," he said. "Now, you need to promise me something."

"What?"

"If you must think about all of this, do it, but don't go out and ask questions." He paused and eyed me. "And stay home as much as possible. I don't want to have to worry about you."

For the first time since that horrible day when I found Jim Bob, I felt a few warm fuzzies for the detective. And his attitude toward me had mellowed. Perhaps I could use this to my advantage. I crossed my arms. "Let's make a deal."

He snorted and shook his head. "Cops don't make deals. Lawyers make deals."

I folded my hands under my chin in proper begging fashion. "Please? All I want you to do is answer some questions for me."

He blinked a couple of times; then he laughed again. "Fine. All right. Ask. But no guarantees."

I grinned. "Okay. Who is Stefanie, really?"

He thought for a moment. "That is a matter of public record, so I can answer. Sybil Lefebvre Ramsey from Poughkeepsie, New York. She's wanted by the FBI."

"Sybil?" I giggled. "Are you for real?"

"Why is that funny?" he asked.

"There's this movie about this woman named Sybil with multiple personalities, and it's just ironic that . . ." I stopped when I realized what he'd said. "Her last name was Ramsey?"

He nodded.

"So Carey, or Peter, or whoever he was, was her husband?"

He nodded again. "Yep. Got it in one."

"She wasn't legally married to Jim Bob?"
"Nope," Detective Scott said.
Alley cat did not begin to describe Stefanie. "Was she a true blond?"
He stared at me as if I was crazy. "I have no idea, although her hair was different in each place she lived."
She was as bad as her husband, disguising herself. "Well, did she murder Peter?"
He shrugged. "Can't answer that."
"Can't or won't?" I asked.
"I can't, and I won't," he said.
That probably meant she hadn't. "Okay, was it true that Peter Ramsey was supposedly dead?"
He nodded. "That's what the public thought, yes. But the FBI didn't believe it. Sybil and Peter's last scam didn't go so well. Their victim figured it out before they could leave, and Peter accosted him. After the two disappeared with thousands, the man died, thus making Peter wanted for murder. But a month later, his belongings were found neatly piled on the railing of a very high bridge with a suicide note. His body was never found. Of course, there was no body to find."
I made a mental note to watch *Mysterious Disappearances* every day. Who knew what I'd learn? "Did you find proof of all of Jim

Bob's blackmailing victims in that unit?"

"That's possible," he said.

"And he had the unit to keep Stefanie from getting into his stuff, right? I mean, the timing of his rental coincides with his marriage."

Detective Scott shrugged. "Probably, but we'll never know for sure."

I frowned. "What, exactly, was she looking for in there? Seems to me, she'd have taken his money and run after he died. . . ." I met Detective Scott's gaze while my mind raced.

Jim Bob had met Stefanie in the Cayman Islands. From what I had heard about Jim Bob, he didn't strike me as a Cayman Island kind of guy. But I knew from movies that those kinds of places had banks where people hid their money.

I grinned. "Never mind. I think I get it. He probably had an offshore bank account and hid the information in his unit."

Detective Scott stood. "I think I've more than fulfilled my side of the bargain. Now promise me you'll stay out of trouble."

"Okay." I got up from the sofa, my muscles protesting mightily. Then I walked him to the front door. Truthfully, I would have agreed even if he hadn't answered any of my questions. He was right. I had a baby inside me to think about. A miracle.

After Detective Scott left, I went nuts trying to find my steno pad. I had to add the information I'd found out. I'd ransacked my bedroom and the kitchen drawers; then I pulled the cushions off the couch. Now I was looking underneath a stack of magazines. I began to pick through them one at a time when I heard steps behind me. I turned.

"Are you looking for this?" Max stood in the doorway, holding my notebook. "Karen found it last night and gave it to me."

She was still trying to get me in trouble. He leaned against the door frame. His black jeans and red shirt made him look breathtakingly handsome, but I didn't let that deter me from my quest.

"Good. I didn't want to have to start over —" I stopped. My mouth opened and shut like a bass. I had just confessed that I was still looking into the mystery.

"You're supposed to be resting," he said softly. "You're incorrigible."

"Yes." I looked at the floor.

"Stubborn."

"Yes." I looked at his feet.

"Persistent."

"That, too." I peeked up at him. He wasn't frowning.

"Detective Scott told me some stuff I want

to add to it."

Max cocked his head and frowned. "When?"

"He came by while you were gone and —"

"You talked to him without a lawyer?" Max demanded.

"Well, it wasn't a big deal. He just wanted me to sign my statement. Then he told me to stay out of trouble and take care of my baby."

Max relaxed a fraction. "What was on the statement?"

"Just my observations from last night." I took a step toward him. "It's okay. I didn't need my snooty lawyer."

"I just don't know . . . ," he said.

I was salivating to write down everything I'd learned. I walked over to him and held my hand out for my list. "Give that to me, Max." I stood on my tiptoes and tried to grab it from him.

With little effort, he kept it out of my reach. "First, I have a surprise for you."

A surprise? I put my arm down and stared at him. I loved surprises, especially from my husband. "What is it?"

"How about a deal, and then I give it to you?"

"A deal?" The second one of the day.

He nodded.

"Okay, what is it?" I was enjoying myself immensely.

He grinned. "The surprise and the notebook in exchange for your promise not to run around and ask questions."

I narrowed my eyes and pretended to consider his request, although doing that wouldn't be hard since I'd already promised Detective Scott the same thing. Then it occurred to me that Max must know what I suspected. "So you don't believe the killer has been found, either?"

He now held the notebook at his side. I could easily have snatched it, but I didn't. The fear and concern that tightened his face and filled his eyes made me want to hug him and tell him everything would be okay.

He shook his head. "Figures you'd figure that out. Eric never came out and said as much, but he did caution me to watch out for you."

"Okay, then." I crossed my arms. "I'll play your game, Mr. Tough Negotiator. But I won't agree to anything without knowing what my surprise is."

He pulled a sheaf of folded papers from his back pocket and handed it to me, along with the notebook.

I dropped that on the sofa and glanced through the papers. Itineraries for cruises.

I looked up at him. "For us? Just you and me?"

"Yes." The sparkling eagerness in his eyes made him look like a little boy. "These are the trips the travel agent said were available in the next few months. I discussed them with the kids today. Karen wouldn't join in, of course, but the rest did. You'll notice stars on some of the pages — those are the ones they thought were the best. Honey, I want us to go away together alone for a week. Soon. I've already talked to our parents and made arrangements for the kids. Now all that's left is for you to choose one."

A week alone with Max on a ship. I could think of nothing more fun. I had two concerns. The first was Karen's reaction. This would only fuel her jealousy. I had to think of a way to counteract that. Maybe Max could take her for the day to her favorite amusement park. The second was my brother. I still had no idea if he was guilty of causing Lindsey's death.

"Don't worry about that," Max said softly.

"What?" I looked up at him.

"The thing with Russ won't affect our trip either way, okay?"

He'd read my mind. "Okay. You have a deal." I put my hand out.

He shook it, even while he narrowed his

eyes. "That was too easy. What are you up to?"

"Nothing, Max. Absolutely nothing. I'm going to be good. I'm going to cook, clean, work, and take care of my family. That's all."

And I meant it. I was going to do everything in my power to keep my part of the deal. I had a baby to think about. Besides, I wanted to be alone with Max more than anything in the world.

19

Gail worked behind the counter as I walked through the door of Doris's Doughnuts. My mother was nowhere in sight. The scent of coffee permeated the air. I inhaled it, thinking resignedly that I had at least a year before I could drink it again. I slowly made my way to the counter, nervous about being here. I'd talked to Daddy earlier, and he'd encouraged me to come here to tell my mother about the baby. He said she'd be happy to find out with her friends. Yeah, she'd be happy to have some drama in front of her friends. I was going to do what he asked, but after her comment about my having plenty of kids already, I wasn't sure how she would react.

"Well, if it isn't the local champion of justice." Gail banged a dish.

I wasn't sure if she meant it or not.

"Doris!" she yelled. "Your daughter has arrived."

Ma came bustling from the back, followed by April May.

"Well, I guess your stomach is feeling better now" — Ma sniffed — "since you finally saw fit to come and see me."

I leaned against the counter. "It's not a problem. The nausea is nothing that the obstetrician can't take care of."

"Kids. Well, you know what I say . . ." She stopped midsentence. Very slowly, she and the two bobbleheads turned to stare at me.

"Obstetrician?" my mother whispered.

She and Gail exchanged glances.

"My, my, you've certainly been busy," Gail announced as though she were a loudspeaker. "Solving crimes and getting knocked up."

My face turned bright red. I knew I should have waited until my mother was at home to tell her.

"Wow!" April May clapped her hands together. "Well, you know, if I had a husband who looked like Max, I'd be pregnant all the time."

Better yet, I should have sent a telegram announcing the news.

My mother slapped April May's arm, but I could tell she was pleased. "This calls for a celebration. Free coffee for everyone." She looked pointedly at me. "Except you, missy.

You'll have a decaf mocha latte with whole milk."

She beamed as she worked and said nothing. I'd have to mark this down on my calendar as the day my mother was momentarily speechless and pleased with me at the same time.

"Guess it's all solved, then," Gail said, eyeing me. "You cornered that strumpet and got her arrested."

Funny how things got exaggerated in the telling. "I didn't exactly corner her. It was more like she cornered —"

"Now Four Oaks will once again be safe," she said. "We can sleep tight knowing we won't be murdered in our beds. What with fingerprints on that knife that was stuck in Jim Bob, they should be able to nail her."

I wasn't even going to try to dissuade her from her opinion that all was well, even though I knew it wasn't.

Ma handed me my latte, still beaming. "Well, I'm sure that police detective is grateful for my daughter's help. Why, just yesterday I was at Shopper's Super Saver getting some sirloin ground when Daryl walked by. I told him he was lucky Trish was on the case. What with his physical injuries and all, I'm sure they were ready to blame him. I mean, what about all those stitches? I'll tell you what. I always knew one day Trish's stubbornness would pay off."

That was news to me, or maybe I had amnesia. I only remembered the times she'd told me my persistence would be the death of her.

Ma put her hands on her hips and stared at me. "Why don't all of you come over to dinner tonight? We can celebrate. You have to eat well now. You're too thin."

I guess too thin is better than holding water and looking puffy. "Thanks, Ma, but I'll have to check with Max. He's with his dad, looking over the new storage facility site outside of Baltimore. Then they were going to meet with some people at the county offices. I don't know when he'll be home."

"Well, you and the kids come on without him," she said, as if I'd already replied in the affirmative. "We'll send dinner home for him."

At least we'd eat well. I headed to a table to sit down. I really wished she'd stop talking about me to people. Daryl might still be guilty. In fact, knowing that Sybil-Stefanie had been married to Peter-Carey would certainly give Daryl some motivation. Jealousy.

I sipped my drink and watched April May

wipe tables. When she got to me, she stopped and sat down. "I'm happy for you."

"Thanks," I said.

"I'm glad some people's marriages are working out. So many around here aren't. Besides Stefanie and Jim Bob, I mean. That was doomed from the start because they were both bad people."

April had a succinct way of putting things. I nodded in agreement, although I knew Jim Bob and Stefanie hadn't really been married.

"I have a new boyfriend." She smiled at me shyly with shiny eyes. "I think maybe he's the one."

"That's wonderful," I said.

"He worked at the landfill under Norm." She leaned toward me. "But he began to suspect things weren't right there. You know, the bad trash being hauled in."

I nodded.

"He went over to work at the Shopper's Super Saver. He's a night manager and might be offered the assistant-manager position."

She looked proud, and though I was pleased, I wondered what that meant for Daryl. He was the assistant manager. Had he been arrested or something?

She shook her head. "Isn't it amazing? I

mean, this is a small town and all this stuff is happening. Can you believe Frank?"

"He always seemed so good," I murmured, still thinking about Daryl.

"Yes. He was in here the other day. Your mother thinks he's guilty as sin." April waved her sponge in the air. "Your mother reminded him that you were helping the police. Then Gail said her granddaughter talked to you and told her all about it."

I wanted to groan.

"I'm sure you know this, but the cops have been all over him like a June bug on a porch light. He's living with his parents, but pretty soon, I reckon he'll be living in jail for stealing. It's only a matter of time. His poor kids." She stood. "Not only did he lose his wife, but he lost his fancy car, and he doesn't have a job." She smiled at me. "You're really lucky, Trish. Your mother keeps telling all of us how she's so glad her kids never did nothing really bad."

As usual, my mother was representing things to people the way she wanted them to be. For all our sakes, I hoped that Russ wasn't guilty. My mother would definitely suffer. She might have to close her store from the humiliation.

That afternoon, Karen didn't come home

from school, and she didn't answer her cell phone. I called Tommy at work.

"Hey, Mom, what's up?" he asked.

"Why didn't you bring Karen home?"

He breathed hard into the phone. "She told me you were picking her up."

That wasn't good news. "She isn't here. Did you talk to her any other time today?"

"I saw her between classes. She was upset because Julie left or something like that."

"Tommy, when we ask you to do something, we expect you to do it." Even as I snapped at him, I knew I was overreacting.

"I'm sorry, Mom." He spoke so fast I knew he felt guilty. "I'll ask around, okay?"

I tried to reach Lee Ann. She wasn't at work or at home. Then I called Max. Fortunately, he had his phone turned on.

"Hi, baby." He sounded so relaxed and happy I hated to tell him that his elder daughter was missing.

"Have you heard from Karen?" I asked.

"No." His voice tightened. "Is something wrong?"

"She didn't come home from school. Tommy said Julie was absent and that upset Karen."

Max inhaled. "I hope they haven't run away together. Listen, I'll call the police; then I'll extricate myself from things here.

I'll be home in about an hour and a half, if I don't get caught in traffic. Rush hour starts around this time. Let me know if you hear from her."

Five horrible minutes later, during which I prayed out loud as I paced the hall, the family room, the kitchen, the living room, and Max's office, the phone rang. Karen's cell phone number appeared on caller ID.

I was furious, yanking the receiver up like I was going to choke it. "Karen?"

"I need a ride home." Her voice sounded belligerent.

I didn't understand how she could be so disaffected. I'd be scared if I knew I'd be facing Max after something like this. "Why didn't you get a ride with Tommy? We've been looking all over for you. Your father is calling the police. Why didn't you come home?"

"Why did he call the police?" She sighed. "I know he's really mad. I'm sorry. Can you pick me up at the library?"

"Yes. I'll be there in twenty minutes. Be waiting for me."

I phoned Max. "Karen's at the library. You can cancel the cops. Sammie and I will run over and get her. We'll be here when you get home."

"Yes. Good." He sounded as mad as I felt.

Vehicles filled the library parking lot. I drove around several times and didn't see Karen, nor did I find a space in which to park. Finally, I left the SUV along the side of the road that ran between the library and the woods.

"Come on," I said to Sammie. "Let's go inside."

I didn't find Karen there, either. Over in the children's section, a gray-haired woman read to a group of children gathered on the floor around her feet, her soothing voice a direct contrast to my racing heart.

"Mommy, can I listen?" Sammie whispered.

Having her entertained would help me a lot. "Yes. I have to find Karen. You stay here. I'll be right back, okay?"

She settled on the floor with the other kids.

Karen was nowhere in the building. I even peered into the men's room. At the desk, I got the immediate attention of a librarian, even though there was a line. Pounding on the counter has that effect on people.

"I'm looking for my daughter. She's supposed to be here." My voice sounded high-pitched and tight. "She's taller than you, with long, blond, curly hair."

The woman nodded. "Yes, she was here

awhile ago. She used the bathroom and then left."

I ran outside, scanning the parking lot, trying to control my panic. No sign of her. Maybe she'd seen my SUV and was waiting for us next to it. I ran over to where I'd parked and noticed a big, wood-trimmed station wagon parked in front of my vehicle, but Karen wasn't there. Something wasn't right.

"Mom?"

At the sound of her voice, my breath gushed out in relief. "Karen?" I turned. She stood on the edge of the woods.

"Where have you been?" I snapped as I walked toward her. "You are so grounded. You might not ever have a life. I can't believe —"

"Mom . . ." Her voice squeaked. "I'm sorry. I didn't know."

"What?" I asked, as I got closer.

That's when I noticed someone standing behind her. Lee Ann. She reached around Karen and held a knife to her throat.

"Don't do anything stupid," she said.

I reached into my purse for my cell phone and miraculously found it.

"Drop your purse and the phone," Lee Ann growled, "or I'll kill her right now."

I did what she said.

20

Lee Ann dragged Karen further back into the woods. I followed. Soon the shrubby growth under the trees and my SUV hid us from sight. Anyone driving by would have to stop and focus to see what was really happening.

"Where's Julie?" I asked softly.

"With her father," Lee Ann said.

Karen's chest heaved with ragged breaths that hissed through her clenched teeth. Tears filled her wide eyes. My body shook, but I locked my knees and squeezed my hands shut to control the movement. I had to stay focused.

"What are you doing, Lee Ann?" I hated the way my voice quavered. "You can't possibly get away with this."

"Maybe. Maybe not. Doesn't matter at this point. That stupid detective is sniffing around my door. Because of you."

The knife shifted at Karen's neck. She

whimpered as it nicked the skin on her throat. I saw red, as my mother would say, and not just blood. A red haze of fury.

"Why is that because of me?" I asked through stiff lips.

"You've been talking to the cops. Your mouthy mother brags about it, even at the grocery store. And Karen here has been keeping me up on everything you're doing. She's so gullible. She hates you, you know." Lee Ann shrugged.

"I don't, Mom," Karen whispered. "I didn't mean it." Large tears rolled down her face.

I wanted to tackle Lee Ann so badly that my body shook. "Is this because of Norm drinking? Are you mad because your marriage is failing and mine isn't?"

She snorted. "Norm isn't drinking. That's just what I told people."

Voices drifted from the library. Little kids and their parents began to spill into the parking lot. Then my cell phone rang on the ground behind me.

"Don't pick that up." Lee Ann grabbed Karen's arm, yanking her behind a tree and out of view.

If I screamed, Karen might die. Rushing Lee Ann was too risky. Not with the knife at Karen's throat.

I shifted my position so I could see them, taking deep breaths, trying to calm my mind. The rings of the phone made me want to scream in frustration and fear, but hysteria wouldn't get us out of this. Karen's eyes watched every nuance of my behavior. I couldn't act afraid. I had to keep Lee Ann talking. Then I could figure out a way to disarm her.

The ringing finally stopped.

"Where did you get that knife?" I asked. "It looks like the one that killed Jim Bob."

She laughed. "Jim Bob didn't die from stabbing. That's just what everybody thinks."

"Mommy? Where are you?" Sammie's shout came from the library.

Karen gasped. I trembled as I peered through the trees and the windows of my SUV. Sammie stood on the library's front stoop, looking for me. I was still, hoping she wouldn't see me. She hopped onto the pavement and headed for my vehicle.

My fingernails dug holes in my palms. Lee Ann swore softly behind me. Then a woman rushed out of the library. I heard the low hum of her voice and the high squeak of Sammie's.

"Don't make a sound," Lee Ann hissed.

Sammie hesitated, then trudged back to

take the woman's hand. They disappeared into the library. I breathed a prayer of thanks. Now, to get me and Karen out of this.

"We're leaving," Lee Ann said.

I turned around.

Fury had twisted her face into an unrecognizable mask. "It won't be long before they call the cops."

"Let Karen go," I begged. "Take me."

"Shut up, Trish. You're driving." She glanced around to make sure no one was looking and pushed Karen from behind the tree to where I stood.

I knew if we got in the car with her we were as good as dead. My mind raced. "Where are we going?"

Lee Ann grinned. "Norm's favorite place. Very lucrative."

It didn't take much imagination to know she meant the landfill.

Lee Ann took the knife from Karen's throat and held it to her back. She motioned for me to get in the passenger door. I stood where I was.

"Get a move on, Trish."

I met Karen's gaze. She nodded ever so slightly, and I tried to figure out what she meant. Next thing I knew, she fell to her hands and knees.

"Get up," Lee Ann kicked her.

Kicking my daughter was Lee Ann's last mistake. I roared and leaped at her.

She shrieked and lifted the knife. It glinted as it arced toward me.

"No!" Karen screamed and grabbed Lee Ann's leg.

The knife missed my arm by an inch. I tackled her, slamming her into a tree. The knife fell from her hand, landing on the dirt with a dull thud. Karen scrabbled for it, but Lee Ann kicked wildly, hitting Karen's hip, knocking her off balance. I grabbed a handful of Lee Ann's hair. She screamed and clawed at my face. Her nail caught my nose.

Sirens blared in the distance, but I ignored them. I'd had enough. Perhaps Lee Ann didn't remember my temper in school or the kids I'd beat up. What she really didn't understand was my desperation to save Karen and my unborn baby.

I twisted a hank of her hair in my hands and hooked my foot on her leg. She fell to her knees. I held her hair tight, wrapped around my fingers, but she kept fighting me, so I punched her in the gut. She groaned and slithered to the ground. I rolled her over onto her stomach. Then I kicked the knife away and knelt, with my knees in her back.

"Karen, get a couple of those bungee hook

things from the car."

She scrambled to the SUV. The sirens came closer, and I prayed they were coming for us. Lee Ann struggled under me, trying to knock me off balance, but I jerked her hair and stayed put.

"I thought we were friends," I said.

She swore at me, calling me horrible things that I couldn't hear clearly over the din in the parking lot.

I glared down at her. "I have a feeling you're guilty of a lot of things, but as far as I'm concerned, the very worst thing you did was threaten to kill my daughter."

Karen handed me two bungee cords. I took them from her and wrapped Lee Ann's hands and feet together.

Red and blue reflections of police-car lights glared on my SUV windows and those of the library.

"Wow, Mom." Karen stared at me like I was a superhero. I smiled at her, and for the first time in months, she smiled in return.

I heard shouts and more sirens.

"Go tell them where we are," I ordered, standing guard over Lee Ann.

The next person I saw was Corporal Nick Fletcher.

He reached my side and looked down at Lee Ann. He took his hat off and scratched his head. "Well now, that's got to be the finest example of hog-tying I've ever seen. Too bad we gotta undo it."

He nodded at two other deputies, who took off my bungee cords and hauled Lee Ann to her feet, efficiently handcuffing her. They walked her away with more gentleness than I thought necessary.

I saw Karen in the parking lot talking with Detective Scott, while a deputy put a blanket around her and bundled her into the front seat of a squad car. She was safe.

That's when my knees gave way.

Corporal Fletcher grabbed me under my arms. "Whoa there, Mrs. C. We gotta get you outta here."

Detective Scott ran toward us shouting, but I couldn't hear him clearly, given that I had those annoying little spots in my vision.

"Fletcher . . . Trish . . . Oh, man." He turned around and yelled for a paramedic.

"Just let me sit," I muttered.

Corporal Fletcher lowered me gently to the ground. I leaned against my SUV.

Then he stood and put his hands on his hips, a wide smile on his lips. "Sarge, I never seen anything like this. She's a little firecracker."

Funny, but I kinda liked the guy despite his profession.

The detective knelt next to me and examined my face. "Are you hurt? You're shaking. Your nose is bleeding."

"I'm fine. Just shook up." I met his gaze, trying to hold my hands still. "Her nail got my nose. I'll probably get cooties."

He took a deep breath. "I'm glad that's all."

I felt the concern in his gaze. "You know what?"

"What?" he asked.

"That car that tailgated me was hers. Max was right as usual. I should have told you about it the first time."

He patted my arm.

"I don't want to go to the hospital," I grumbled. "They're going to start charging me rent."

He shrugged. "They won't take you if you don't need to go, but I do want you and Karen checked out."

"Well, I have to call Max. He's going to kill me anyway, so maybe we should wait until then."

Detective Scott smiled. "We can't wait. I just talked to him. He's stuck in Baltimore rush hour traffic."

I swallowed. "I guess he's not very happy."

He shook his head. "That's putting it mildly, but he does know you're both alive."

The paramedics arrived. The detective stood. He and Corporal Fletcher moved out of their way.

"Detective Scott," I called as they arranged me on the stretcher.

"Yes?"

"This wasn't something I did on purpose. I didn't break my promise."

"I know."

Max stopped in the doorway of the family room, tie undone, hair mussed, staring at me and Karen as if seeing a vision. His chest moved with short, uneven breaths. Then he crossed the room, holding out his arms. "Both of you come here."

We did. He grabbed our shoulders and kissed the tops of our heads. "When I couldn't reach either of you, I almost lost my mind," he whispered. "I was so worried. All I could do was pray. I didn't know what I'd do if . . ."

I stood on my toes and put my lips on his cheek. It felt wet and tasted salty. Maxwell Cunningham the Third, my husband, the love of my life, was crying.

I looked over his shoulder where my mother and father stood, watching. They had come to pick up Charlie and Sammie. For the second time this week, my mother didn't say a word.

Detective Scott arrived shortly after, and Max brought him into the family room.

Karen and I were huddled under blankets on the couch. I'd tried to tell Max that I was hot and didn't need to be covered, but he ignored me.

"I'm sorry," the detective said. "I wish I could have acted faster. I had a feeling Lee Ann was getting ready to leave town, especially when she sent Julie away to meet Norm. I was working with the DA to put together an arrest warrant."

Max sat next to me and put his arm around my shoulders. As much as I loved being near him, I was sweating from the combination of the blanket and his body heat.

"I need a statement from you tonight," Detective Scott said.

Karen spoke first. Lee Ann had called and begged Karen for a meeting. Julie had supposedly run away, and Lee Ann wanted Karen's opinions about where Julie had gone.

I managed to wriggle the blanket off while Karen talked, but I couldn't escape Max's arm — not that I wanted to.

"We talked in her car in the parking lot," Karen said. "Then she told me I should call

Mom to come and get me. She'd wait with me and explain." Karen swallowed. "After I called, I went to the bathroom and came back outside to wait with her. That's when I started to realize something was wrong."

Max's arm had tightened on my shoulders as Karen spoke.

"Mrs. Snyder had already said something about Mom smashing Peter's head in, but I thought she was sort of joking." Karen glanced at me. "She did say that Mom had been a violent maniac in school and had everyone fooled that she'd changed."

Sounded to me like Lee Ann took advantage of an already angry child. I still couldn't comprehend that she could pretend to be my friend and hate me that much.

I wiggled in Max's too-tight grasp as he looked at Karen. He loosened his hold. "What do you think now?"

Karen wouldn't look at us. "I . . . don't believe it. Mom told Mrs. Snyder to take her and leave me. She was going to die for me." Her voice broke.

I put my arms around her. We had a lot to work out, but this was a start.

Detective Scott asked me to explain what happened at the library, which I did. Then I asked Karen to go upstairs and take a hot bath. I had a couple of things to ask the detective that I didn't want her to hear.

After she was gone, I met his gaze. "I know Jim Bob wasn't killed with the knife. I think he was already dead when he was stabbed, probably by Frank, since he was so terribly concerned about the knife and acted like he wanted to point the finger at a meat cutter. Big, fat tattletale. I think Lee Ann killed Jim Bob. Maybe with that hammer I told you about. Remember what Lee Ann told Karen about me smashing in Peter-Carey's head?"

Detective Scott said nothing. Neither did Max.

"Well?" I asked.

The detective stood. "I'm not at liberty to discuss any of that."

The statement was so like him that I laughed.

21

That evening would be forever etched in my mind, as I'm sure it would be in Karen's. God had used a bad situation for good. Since that night, Karen and I had reached an understanding of sorts. She finally understood how much I loved her, but the emotions that had been driving her hadn't totally disappeared. During our first emergency counseling session with the pastor, I realized the anger she directed at me was misplaced. She was really angry that God had allowed her real mother to die, and for some reason, it had taken this long to surface.

Max's PI hadn't discovered anything about Russ, Lindsey, or the stop sign. I had to admit a certain feeling of satisfaction, although I really wanted to know.

I picked out my cruise. Almost a month later, when the time drew near, I began to make lists, which I promptly lost. I had to buy clothes. That wasn't one of my favorite things to do. Especially dressy ones. I'm a jeans and sweatshirt kind of girl. But when I saw the red evening gown at the mall, I knew it was perfect. Given the cut and how it fell just right, I was pretty sure Max would get that gleam in his eyes when he saw it, so I'd keep it a secret until I wore it on the ship.

I had two errands to do on my way home. The first was a visit to the sheriff's office to see Detective Scott. He'd called and requested that I come by. Being back in the building made me sweat. I felt immediately guilty, even though I'd done nothing. I told the guy behind a glass window that I was there to see Detective Scott. He told me to be seated, but it wasn't long before the detective himself came to get me. After he greeted me, he led me back into the inner sanctum and up the stairs and surprised me when he didn't lead me to the interview room. Instead, he took me to his office.

"Have a seat, please," he said.

I settled into a chair and put my purse on the floor. On the credenza behind him was a picture of a girl who looked to be high school age. I saw no picture of a wife. I guessed he hadn't remarried.

I turned my gaze on him and saw a smile

on his face.
He tapped a folder on his desk. "I have some good news for you."
Was it possible? I leaned forward. "Russ?"
Detective Scott nodded. "Yes. I don't think he did it."
I began to cry, something I'd been more prone to since I'd gotten pregnant.
Detective Scott handed me a tissue.
"Who did it?" I sniveled.
"We suspect Tim, Daryl's brother. But my first lead came from an interesting source."
"Who?" I asked as I wiped my nose.
"You. Then your parents."
That dried up my tears. "What?"
He grinned. "You'd mentioned that box of doughnuts your mother delivered to Jim Bob. I had to follow up on that, although I didn't suspect her, so I went to your parent's house to chat. Your father was there. When she broke down and confessed, he got upset and asked her why she never told him. She said, like you, she'd seen the stop sign and thought Russ had done it. Your father informed both of us that Tim Boyd had given the sign to Russ. After several meetings with Daryl, where I tried to, er, convince him to tell me the truth, he finally admitted that he suspected his brother, too."
Poor Daryl probably confessed because

he had been tortured by the tapping of Detective Scott's pen, just like I had been. And I found it just a little disturbing that my mother and I had both been threatened by the same person and kept it a secret from our husbands. I did not want to be like my mother. I looked at Detective Scott. "So what happens now?"

He sighed. "Case closed. Tim is dead. I told Max this morning and asked him to let me tell you. He's going to tell Lindsey's parents. He doesn't think they'll want any publicity."

I was sure, too. Lindsey's parents were friends of the Cunninghams and, like them, despised bad publicity. My heart ached for them. And for Max.

"Thank you," I said.

"You're welcome."

I shifted in my chair. "Can you answer some questions for me while I'm here?"

He briefly tapped his pen on the desk then put it down. "I still can't answer everything, but I'll tell you what I can."

"That'll do," I said. "What's going on with Frank?"

"He's been charged with embezzlement. Since he stabbed a dead guy, we can't charge him with murder. And since he thought Jim Bob was alive, he can't be charged with messing with a corpse or a crime scene."

"I'll bet lawyers said that. It's full of loopholes." I thought about Calvin Schiller.

Detective Scott laughed. "Yep."

"What about Lee Ann?" I bit my lip. I'd begun to feel guilty that I hadn't seen the whole thing coming and somehow prevented it. Despite what she'd done, I couldn't forget all the time we'd spent together.

Eric shook his head. "We have enough evidence to prove that she killed two men. She's been arrested, as has Norm, for the landfill fiasco."

"Ah," I said. "Jim Bob was blackmailing her about the landfill, wasn't he? I'll bet he found out somehow from April's boyfriend. Lee Ann smashed Jim Bob with that hammer, didn't she?"

Detective Scott shook his head. "I'm listening."

"And she and Norm were running away, weren't they? I think he made money in paybacks at the landfill for accepting out-of-state trash." I laid my arms on his desk. "Then Peter-Carey started threatening her like he did me, so she killed him, right?" I paused.

"I'm still listening," the detective said.

Would he answer any of my questions? I'd try something else. "How did Jim Bob's body get behind the milk?"

"Well, it's still a matter of some speculation on my part." He eyed me. "And please don't talk about this with anyone, okay?"

At least he finally trusted me to keep my word.

"We think Lee Ann lost her temper with Jim Bob and whacked him with the hammer that she was taking to Daryl. She didn't think she'd killed him at first." He squinted at me. "She must have left Jim Bob somewhere in a back room. When she checked on him again, he was dead. That's where Frank comes in.

"Frank was on a rampage about knives. He was adamant about keeping things in their proper place, so perhaps he was taking one back to where it belonged in the meat department. He saw Jim Bob, thought he was unconscious, and stabbed him. Then he put him on that cart and wheeled him somewhere to keep him hidden."

"Didn't either one of them think they'd be caught?" I asked. "Sounds stupid."

Detective Scott grinned. "That's what makes my job easier. If crooks were smart, we wouldn't be able to catch them. Besides, much of the staff was absent that morning with the flu. That made hiding Jim Bob a lot easier."

"Well, how did Jim Bob end up behind the milk?"

"We think Lee Ann looked for him and finally found the cart. When she saw that he'd been stabbed, she shoved the cart into the cold room where he could be found easily. She hoped the police would think he'd been stabbed to death and that his head had been bashed as he fell."

I thought about Lee Ann and the possible things that had driven her to the point of murder. I looked at my finger and bit at my nail. "I feel bad about all this. I keep wondering if there was anything I could have done differently. Maybe if I'd been closer to Lee Ann in recent years, she would have talked instead of killing. And poor Frank. He's annoying and all, but when I beat him up in school, do you think I messed up his mind?"

Detective Scott shook his head. "One thing I can say without any hesitation. This was not your fault. I've seen a lot in my job, more bad than good, I'm afraid. Maybe you weren't the kindest person when you were young. Maybe you've made some mistakes, but I can say without a doubt that you're one of the good people." He grinned.

"Maybe a little stubborn and impetuous, but still very nice."

I blinked. Had he just said something sweet to me?

He stood. "Don't look so surprised. I can be nice, too."

"Thank you." I grabbed my purse and jumped to my feet. "I have to finish packing. Max is taking me on a cruise for a whole week."

"I heard. Please have fun. You deserve it after all this. Now you can leave it all behind. When you come back, your life can return to normal."

I wasn't sure I wanted my life to return to normal. I didn't like my kids being threatened, or even me, but I did like making mystery lists and thinking about them.

He walked around his desk and picked up something from the floor. "You might want this."

I took my phone from his hand. He walked me out the door and stood there as I walked down the hall. I had a thought and turned around. "Next time, I'll let you see my notebook," I said. "It was quite thorough, if I do say so myself."

His mouth fell open. "Next time?"

I didn't answer, just turned around and chuckled all the way to my car.

My visit with Eric left me in a good frame of mind to deal with the next thing I needed to face. Before I could truly leave things behind, I had to beat my foe. The milk case at the Shopper's Super Saver. I hadn't been back since the murder.

I hurried to the back of the store to get it over with. As I stood in front of the glass doors, looking at gallons of milk, I remembered that horrible morning. Poor Jim Bob. He had been a very nasty man, but no one deserved to die like that.

"Trish?"

I whirled around. "Daryl."

He wore the red Shopper's Super Saver manager's jacket. He'd gotten a promotion. Dweeb that he'd been, I suddenly saw what Abbie meant. He wasn't bad as men went, although he wasn't Maxwell Cunningham by any stretch of the imagination. Strangely, Daryl's new position fit him. I found myself hoping that maybe some new self-respect would help him be more confident in his marriage.

"Hi," I said and glanced behind me at the milk. "This is the first time I've been back since . . . you know."

He nodded. "Why don't you take three gallons of milk free for your pain. And . . ." He sighed. "As an apology for the road sign thing. I'm sorry. I was trying to protect my brother's reputation."

Who was I to throw stones, as my mother would say. I had done the same. "It's over now, Daryl. And I'm sorry, too."

"Listen, Trish —" He moved closer to me. "I owe you big time, and not just for that."

"For what?"

He glanced around. "Well, I know that without your help, I might have been arrested for Jim Bob's murder. My fingerprints were on that hammer. I was hanging certificates in my office that morning. I managed to break some glass while I was at it, as well as smash my thumb."

Another answer to a question. That's why he'd been at the doctor's office. "You know, Daryl, I didn't help with the investigation. I was a suspect, too. I mean —"

"Don't be modest. Your mother has been telling everyone what you did." He smiled at me. "You're a real sleuth."

Moonlight over the ocean is one of the most romantic sights in the world, especially wrapped in the arms of a man like Max. I leaned back against his chest, and his arms tightened around my shoulders.

I loved our cozy little deck. Although we'd attended a fancy dinner with the captain tonight, we'd eaten most of our meals out here alone, watching the water, discussing topics as mundane as our favorite cheeses and as complicated as world politics. We explored our faith, grateful to God for what we had and for each other. I had my wish — time alone with Max. Without guilt.

This was better than a honeymoon. No newlywed nerves to get over or awkwardness to work through. In the familiarity, we'd discovered things about each other that we'd never known before.

"Baby, are you happy?" Max nibbled my neck.

"Mmm."

"Your dress makes me crazy." He kissed my ear.

I smiled to myself. The red gown did exactly what I'd hoped.

He laid a hand on my stomach. "You haven't been sick since we left."

"No coffee. I feel really good." Content. Peaceful.

"I'm happy, too," he said. "Having another baby seems right, somehow. Like confirmation of how much I love you. Of our love for each other and God's love for us."

He couldn't have said anything nicer. I extricated myself from his arms and turned around to face him. His black tuxedo and my dress added a dash of sophistication and mysteriousness to the night, like we were the hero and heroine in one of Abbie's novels. I ran his lapels between my fingers. Talk about making someone crazy. Nobody looks better in a suit than Max. I glanced up at his face.

He smiled and touched my cross necklace. "You're still wearing it."

"It means as much to me as my wedding ring," I said, thinking how much Max meant to me and how grateful I was to God for him and my family.

He ran a finger over my lips. "I'm glad it's all over." His eyes looked fathomless in the moonlight.

"What's over?" I murmured as I kissed his neck.

"Murder and mayhem. Police investigations."

"Oh. That." I didn't want to admit to Max that I missed writing down clues.

He pulled me closer. I leaned my head against his chest, listening to the solid thump of his heart and sighed with pleasure. No interruptions. No children knocking at the door. No ringing phones. Just me and Max.

"And no more mystery lists." He stepped back, looked me up and down, and his eyes gleamed. "How about let's go inside."

I smiled. All of Max's attention was on me. As single-minded as he was, that made for lots of fun. I, however, was more easily distracted, even from him for once. As we stepped back into our cabin, I told myself that when I got home, I was going to buy more steno pads, which were easy to use and transport. Maybe something would come up. I sort of liked solving mysteries.

ABOUT THE AUTHOR

Candice Speare denies rumors that she's slightly eccentric. When she's not working or writing, Candice exercises and fiddles on the computer. She is mom to one daughter, who is married to a sailor in the U.S. Navy.

You may correspond with this author by writing:

Candice Speare
Author Relations
PO Box 721
Uhrichsville, Ohio 44683

The employees of Thorndike Press hope you have enjoyed this Large Print book. All our Thorndike, Wheeler, and Kennebec Large Print titles are designed for easy reading, and all our books are made to last. Other Thorndike Press Large Print books are available at your library, through selected bookstores, or directly from us.

For information about titles, please call:
(800) 223-1244

or visit our Web site at:
http://gale.cengage.com/thorndike

To share your comments, please write:
Publisher
Thorndike Press
295 Kennedy Memorial Drive
Waterville, ME 04901